A MURDER AT THE COUNTRY CLUB
A CANTERBURY GOLF CLUB MYSTERY
BOOK 1

BY: JESSA ARCHER

On the night of the Canterbury Golf Club's First Annual Glow-ball Golf Tournament, Lady Captain Beatrice Yates argues with Rudolph "Ruddy" Agani in front of all the members and specially invited guests because Ruddy can't get along with anyone. When Ruddy is found murdered on the club's seventeenth hole soon after, Beatrice becomes the prime suspect. Even her best friend and golf partner, Trudi, struggles to defend her.

But Beatrice is not the only golfer who wanted to bash Ruddy over the head with a niblick. Ruddy was a stingy old coot and owed plenty of people in the small town money that he could've paid back, and he had carried those penny-pinching ways over to the club's finances, too. The list of suspects looks like Saturday morning's tee times schedule.

With her best friend, Trudi, and her cantankerous uncle Arnie at her side, retired kindergarten-teacher Beatrice is prepared to play the whole course to solve the mystery, find the killer, and repair the club's reputation before money problems force her cherished club to close.

D1520310

Don't let Jessa's new books be a mystery to you!
Sign up for Jessa Archer's New Release Alerts
at jessaarcher.com

PRAISE FOR JESSA ARCHER'S OTHER MYSTERIES

"I just love these cozy mysteries! This was another very well-done story in this series with twists and turns to keep the reader moving through those pages! Grab your copy and see how quickly you can figure out the murderer!" ~~ Emily, Top 500 Amazon Reviewer

"This mystery was extremely well done. The plot twists and the scandals were fun!" ~~ PagePrincess Blog

"I am so enjoying this series! And not just because the heroine, amateur sleuth Jamie Lang and I share the same first name! I love the hand lettering aspects of it, as I am a calligrapher myself. (I find myself wondering if the author herself has a love of lettering, because two series of hers now have had to do with it in some way, this one on hand lettering and another on typography.) I love how Jamie notices details, like a woman in her profession would. In this book, the author strikes the perfect balance between cozy and mystery. What do I mean by that? Some cozy mysteries put too much emphasis on the interesting characters or community, and the mystery lags (or is too obviously solved). Others have the opposite problem. Ms. Archer strikes the perfect balance between the two. I love the story. What a method of murder in general, and in particular for such a master lettering craftsman as the victim. I also enjoy a mystery with a lot of potential suspects, and this one had plenty. The book pulled me right into the story's world, and I loved watching the details unfold. Another excellent book in this series." ~~ Amazon Reviewer

ALSO BY JESSA ARCHER

"The Mystery of the Missing Crystal Golf Ball"
A Murder at the Country Club
A Murder at the Devil's Ball (Halloween Murder Mystery)

Look for ALL the Jessa Archer Mysteries at Jessa's
website!

Legal Beagle Mysteries
Hand Lettering Calligraphy Mysteries
Coastal Playhouse Mysteries
Canterbury Golf Club Mysteries
Hidden Harbor Tea Shop
Tink Tank Knitting Mysteries

A MURDER AT THE COUNTRY CLUB

A CANTERBURY GOLF CLUB MYSTERY
BOOK 1

Jessa Archer

ARCHER PUBLISHING

First Print Edition: September, 2019

Printed in the United States of America

Get notices of new releases,
special discounts, freebies, and
deleted scenes and epilogues
from Jessa Archer!

Sign Up for Jessa Archer's Email List
http://smarturl.it/jessa

A MURDER AT THE COUNTRY CLUB

A CANTERBURY GOLF CLUB MYSTERY
BOOK 1

CHAPTER 1

RUDOLPH "RUDDY" AGANI was murdered on the green of
the Canterbury Golf Club's seventeenth hole during the First
Annual Nighttime Glow-Ball Golf Tournament, but no one
saw who killed him.

Everyone saw Ruddy leave the party in the clubhouse
two hours before, of course.

No one could have missed it.

Not the members, not the guests we were trying to
impress, and not the local newspaper photographer.

Every eye in the clubhouse swiveled and watched Ruddy
stomp out, muttering and bobbling his close-cropped head in
anger, right after they had seen me give him a stern dressing
down.

Later, as four of us stood over Ruddy's dead body in the
dark, shining the flashlights from our cell phones at the wine-
dark stain on the shaved grass while the corpse's motionless
hand reached for the flagpole that whipped in the breeze,

everyone turned and looked at me.

I was as shocked as everyone else that someone had killed Ruddy, though.

No one expects a murder at a country club.

CHAPTER 2

THE FIRST ANNUAL Nighttime Glow-Ball Golf Tournament was held at the Canterbury Golf Club in early May.

Though May should have been late spring in New England, the golfers wore thick undershirts, pullovers, and sturdy, woolen socks for the social outing. The breeze blew stiffly, pulling at everyone's clothes, and the chill felt more like March that evening.

Despite the chilly weather, we had played three holes of golf in the pitch-black dark with glowing balls that had striped like meteors down the dark fairways and putted them into the glowing holes on the greens. Lighted poles had marked the edges of the fairways so people didn't get lost out there. The course had a good number of trees that were tall hulks in the deep night.

The brisk air and walk in the dark had been amusing and exhilarating, and our foursome had shot a respectable fifty-two among us. The leaderboard charts hanging on the wall in the clubhouse showed that other groups had done better and so would win.

The point of the outing was not to win.

At least, it wasn't for me.

As the golfers came in from playing their three-hole rounds in the dark, the clubhouse became packed with people sipping drinks and eating hors d'oeuvres off tiny, china plates.

Laughter, talking, and classic rock music filled the clubhouse, and the members and guests seemed to be having a good time as I shimmied between crowded groups, chatting and sizing up the crowd.

The clubhouse was packed full of members and guests.

Members had been required to bring guests to this festive outing.

Yes, *required.*

The members and guests had arrived earlier in the evening for supper before the glow-ball tournament, while the sun had still lingered above the horizon and they could enjoy the spectacular golf course panorama beyond the clubhouse's windows.

On the golf course, the trees were mostly leafed out after the long winter that year, and the grass was thick and manicured to show our club off at its best advantage to the guests. Indeed, the fairways had been spotless without a downed leaf nor a blade of grass out of place. The rough had been cut to a length that seemed proper but not punitive, and the sand traps were raked in pleasing patterns.

We needed those guests to admire the Canterbury Golf Club.

We needed them to *join* the Canterbury Golf Club.

The Canterbury Golf Club needed new members desperately. The rival golf club only ten miles away and one town over, the Greens of Grass Country Club, had poached five dozen of our members during the winter months with a no-initiation-fee special and reduced dues for two years. The Canterbury Ways and Means Committee had had a nasty surprise when the members' spring dues did not roll in this year.

Suddenly, Canterbury's bank accounts weren't quite so flush with cash as they had been in decades past, but the bills still arrived daily.

The club's recent insolvency was a closely held secret among the people who managed the club, like myself. I am Beatrice Yates, and I have been the Lady Captain for five years, which meant I knew a great deal about the club that the regular rank-and-file members did not.

For example, I knew that the greenskeeper, Bhagwan Das, overwatered the greens, and the club's monthly water bill was astronomical.

I knew that certain club members must be padding their handicaps, a practice called *sandbagging*, which is a deplorable method of cheating at golf. My eighty-three-year-old uncle, Arnie Holmes, was certainly one of them, and sandbagging was not the only way he massaged his scores. Luckily, Uncle Arnie over-tipped the waitstaff and tended to buy lunches and bar rounds for his friends and others, so no one had murdered him yet.

And I knew that if at least forty-three new members were not admitted into the Canterbury Golf Club by the end of the fall, the golf club would be forced to close and sell the golf course, clubhouse, and sundry bits to the local town of Canterbury for far less than they were worth, due to a clause in the initial purchase contract, seven decades earlier.

The town would turn this gracious track into a muni.

If that happened, this private, modestly priced golf club wouldn't be the same, and yet one more piece of my much-loved and very-missed husband would be gone.

So, I didn't want that to happen.

As Lady Captain, I was in somewhat of a position to help save the club.

Thus, I was throwing golfing soirees and outings and lunches and trying to lure prospective members into joining up. We needed only a few dozen people, and Canterbury was a very nice course and club. I thought of my tasks as spreading the joy of golf.

The evening of the glow-ball tournament was proceeding brilliantly, and my fellow board members and staff had whispered to me that twenty people had inquired about membership that evening.

Not that I was counting them on my fingers and toes or

anything.

The happy babble of the crowd with occasional surges of laughter rolled through the clubhouse. Glasses clinked. Heads of brown, black, auburn, blond, silver, and salted pepper leaned toward each other in conversation.

The ladies' golf pro, Sherlynne Orman, stood at the front of the room, carefully inking scores on the leaderboard in calligraphic numbers as foursomes came in from the course. One of our hostesses, Melanie, was reading the scores to her from cards while members and guests clustered around them, cheering as each number went up.

Over on the other side of the room, trouble brewed.

I could sense the disturbance in the room even before the grumble of angry voices reached me.

As a thirty-year veteran of kindergarten classrooms, I had sixth, seventh, and eighth senses for when things were going wrong and about to devolve into a slap fight.

The back corner of the room rippled with angry tones that were rising over the conversation, and the people around the two men who were involved in the disagreement were growing silent and shuffling away in concern.

I leaped through the crowd, parting the humans and dodging tables and juice boxes—*er*, cocktails—to reach the two grown men who were arguing in the corner.

The crowd tightened as people were backing away from Rudolph "Ruddy" Agani and Oliver Shwetz.

Ruddy's face was once again flushed in anger, color

rising in his cheeks and nose. Despite the fact that Ruddy's given name was Rudolph, people assumed that his nickname was a reference to the way his face reddened whenever he was angry, which was often. Ruddy's fists clenched at his sides near the seams of his pants, and he was leaning forward as if to force his sneer toward Oliver.

Oliver Shwetz, however, was leaning back with his arms tightly crossed over his chest and his eyebrows pinched in anger. He scowled, and his gaze flicked from Ruddy, who seemed about to attack, to the crowd staring at them. Oliver was shaking his head, his lips pursed together as if he was not going to say one more word.

As Oliver denied whatever Ruddy was accusing him of, Ruddy's hound-like face reddened more. Though he was perhaps in his mid-fifties, brown streaked the whites of his eyes like a morose man of nine decades or a person prone to rages so intense that anger had broken blood vessels in his eyes.

Everyone who had dealt with Ruddy knew which one he was.

I reached the two men and raised my hands. Years of being the sole adult in a room full of five-year-olds served me well. "Gentlemen," I announced, "may I see you in my office, please?"

"That won't be necessary." Ruddy hissed the last word. "Oliver was just apologizing, and I was leaving. I need to talk to someone."

A Murder at the Country Club

And then Ruddy stomped to the double doors, flung one open and let it bang the wall, and stormed out of the clubhouse, nearly bowling over three golfers coming in from the dark course.

CHAPTER 3

EVERYONE WATCHED RUDDY Agani leave the clubhouse and march into the darkness.

One of the people coming in through the double doors, Pauline Damir, stumbled as Ruddy shoved her out of his way, and she dropped her green, glowing golf ball. It rolled away on the carpeting.

A chain of club members passed it back to her. People patted her shoulders, checking on her, but she insisted she was fine even though she glared outside the wide windows with a truly angry expression. "That Ruddy Agani is a jerk," Pauline was heard to mutter to the woman who held her elbow with concern. "I could just strangle him."

Her husband, Tom, pushed through the crowd to make sure she was all right.

The members and guests that filled the clubhouse swiveled and watched Ruddy flounce out, including the reporter from the *Canterbury Tales,* the local town newspaper, who raised her camera and snapped a picture of Ruddy's back as he marched out the back doors, snarling at people who then immediately backed away from him.

White light flashed over the crowd.

The reporter, Lale Kollen, lowered her camera. "Well, that was exciting. Does that happen often at the Canterbury Country Club?"

"*Golf club*, Canterbury *Golf Club*, though we have tennis courts and a pool, too," I corrected her absently as I stepped forward to check on Oliver. Getting the name right in the newspaper article was important for our publicity efforts. "No, of course, it doesn't. Oliver, are you all right?"

Oliver Shwetz seemed to shake himself like he was flicking the anger off of his shoulders. "I'm fine. Thank you, Beatrice, but I'm fine. I'll drown my sorrows in the shrimp and cocktail sauce."

With no more opportunity to watch a fight, the crowd collectively turned their backs and resumed chatting. Even Lale, the newspaper reporter, wandered away to take pictures of the way the candlelight was glinting on the crystal punch bowl.

Hopefully, Lale would take pictures of all the happy people doing fun things, I mused. We didn't want the one little scuffle to be the focus of the article about the Canterbury Golf Club.

I turned back to Oliver. "Are you sure you don't want to decompress in my office for a bit?"

A Murder at the Country Club

Oliver Shwetz sighed. "Maybe that's a good idea. My cardiologist said that stress is going to give me a heart attack someday, if this doesn't do it first." He patted his round belly. "He says I should quit my law firm, too."

Oliver had been Canterbury's general-practice attorney for decades. Whether you needed to sue an insurance company over a fender-bender, sell your house, or write your will, he was the lawyer for the job. He also gave discounts to club members. I told him, "Well, I have enjoyed getting out more since I retired. More time for golf."

His smile was a little wan, and he leaned in as he frowned. "Maybe I should retire. Maybe it is getting to be too much for me. I'm making stupid mistakes."

I patted him on the shoulder. "I'm sure it's nothing, Oliver. You know where my office is, upstairs. Go do some meditating and lower that blood pressure a bit. Take deep breaths and think about golf."

Oliver perked up a little. "I had a good round this morning."

"Yes, muse on that."

He left me standing in the crowd, and I bustled off to find my uncle Arnie Holmes and talk to him about how the night was going. He'd been several groups behind Pauline Damir and her foursome, so he should have been finishing his three holes of glow-ball golf soon. I just had to wait for him to come into the clubhouse.

If anyone knew all the gossip in the club, my uncle

would.

It took me half an hour to work my way through the crowd, talking to old friends who were members and chatting with the prospectives because we wanted their money.

One woman wanted to know if some of the appetizers were gluten-free. I had discussed this with Chef Leopold earlier, so I knew what to tell her. "Everything except the meatballs and the teriyaki skewers is gluten-free. The chef is very careful about cross-contamination. Try the cheese mini-soufflés, deviled eggs, cucumber rounds, and veggie platters."

Other prospectives wanted to know when the pool would be open. I told them in late June, and then they wanted to know if there were adult-only times because that's when the kids got out of school. Yes, we had adult swim times.

Another possible member wanted to discuss the tennis courts. I discussed like a champ. We needed every new member we could get.

I dodged around the golf club's trophy case, a glass and steel shelving unit packed with trophies that our teams had brought home from tournaments plus valuable pieces of golf memorabilia, like a crystal golf ball that had once belonged to the great golfer Bobby Jones—but that's a different story. The case divided the main part of the dining room from a small passage on the edge, mostly used by the wait staff during restaurant hours. We still needed to outfit the trophy case with glass doors and locks to protect the items on the shelves. As I was the club's Lady Captain, I should probably arrange that. Everything fell under my purview.

My best friend in the whole world, Trudi von Shike, was standing in a corner alone behind the trophy case, checking something on her phone. Her short, gray hair had swung forward, curtaining the sides of her face, and she looked like a wiry little imp who might spring up and vault to the chandelier to gambol above the crowd.

Some people go through their whole lives, wondering who would be there for them if anything devastating happened. I knew who my real friends were. In a world of acquaintances, Trudi was *real*. We'd been friends for more than thirty years, since our college days, and when things had been rough for me, Trudi had been there every day.

I asked her, "How's it going?"

"Oh, fine," Trudi said, slipping her phone into her back pocket. "Just introverting for a minute. The night seems to be going well."

I dropped my head to whisper, "Other than Oliver and Ruddy nearly brawling."

"Yeah, Ruddy's a jerk at Accounting Board meetings, too."

"I'm worried their little scene will deter some of the guests who might be considering a membership," I whispered to her.

Trudi wrinkled her nose and swished her hand in the air. "Oh, Bee. Tomorrow, no one will remember that scuffle even happened. Look at all of them. Everyone's having a great time. They'll remember the amazing glow-ball golf and the fantastic steak and lobster for supper, not to mention the potato gratin. Chef Leo did an amazing job with that. I heard that another five people picked up membership packets in the last half-hour. I restocked the packet table because so many people were snagging one, and almost no one has gone home yet. Most interested guests will probably grab packets on their way out, rather than lug them around all night."

Trudi served on several of the club's committees, including Ways and Means, Accounting, Regulatory Compliance, and Greens. She knew about the club's money problems and the soggy grass, too.

"I'm hoping for fifteen new memberships from this outing," I told Trudi, still whispering. "If we can make that, we'll be back on track."

She bit her lip. "It's possible. We'll have to see how many sit-downs we book in the next few weeks."

"Right. Did you see where Uncle Arnie went?"

"He came in a few minutes ago and went straight to the bar." She sighed. "Well, I suppose I'd better mingle and be friendly to the people who might give us their money. Plus, socialization increases serotonin levels. So, there's that."

Trudi trudged into the crowd to do her social duty and increase her serotonin levels.

I shook hands and hugged my way through the crowd

and into the bar, where the lights were dimmer and the crowd was sparser. A few people loitered while the bartender made special orders, but waiters roved through the crowd with glasses of beer and wine.

Uncle Arnie was standing with a group of the older ladies and gents who were club members, back in a dark corner of the bar away from the DJ.

Four, long, white hairs covered his bald pate, more speckled with sun damage the last few years because he had started wearing mesh hats. His little clutch of people was grousing about something political or social by the way they were holding their glasses in front of their mouths, so I couldn't read their lips as I approached. I'd warned him to be on his good behavior for the prospective members that night. "Arnie, honey? What's the news?"

He set his empty glass on the polished, mahogany bar, and ice clinked in the crystal. "Evening to ya, Bee. Word is that people liked the glow balls. Ann lost hers, though. We hunted for it for ten minutes before we went on. Maybe have Bhagwan trim the rough a little closer before the glow-ball tournament next year."

The ladies and gents around him nodded, bobbing over their highball glasses.

That was weird. "I'm surprised anyone could lose their glowing ball in the dark like that. They were very easy to find when I tried them out last week."

"Yeah, well, Ann isn't known for hitting them straight.

Other people would like to see nine holes next year instead of three."

It was a compliment, not a complaint, and I smiled at him. "Okay, good. The entertainment board will discuss more holes next year."

Nine holes would have taken too long, and Arnie and his companions would have complained about bedtime.

Maybe we could play six holes next year, though.

If the club still existed next year.

I asked him, "How did your group do?"

"Oh, we did well enough," Uncle Arnie said, preening. "We aren't in the money, but we did respectably, especially considering only three of us finished the three holes."

Yes, Arnie's score probably had been a little more respectable than it should have been. I had sent him off with Ann Carmo, Thorny Williams, and Pauline Damir, none of whom would mind when Arnie modified their scores a bit, too.

Golf reveals character, and it always revealed that Arnie was an intensely competitive, morally flexible old badger who stopped just short of taking other people's money.

Just barely short of it, though.

I loved my uncle and helped him out, but I wouldn't have let him hold onto my credit card without supervision.

Uncle Arnie rolled his glass between his palms and whispered to me, frowning, "The bar is running out of Glenmorangie Eighteen."

A Murder at the Country Club

I covered my heart with my hand in mock horror. "Oh, heavens. There will be panic in the streets."

"We're also out of Pacifico and Lord Hobo Boomsauce."

Which meant the bar was low on several of our best-selling beverages. "Well, then it *is* an emergency. I'll see what I can do."

I consulted with the bartender, received a lengthy shopping list, and trotted out into the dining room. While I was joking with my uncle Arnie, we didn't want the prospective members to find slim pickings at the bar, so I hustled toward my office upstairs.

Members and prospective members asked me questions as I walked by again, and of course, I had to answer or discuss all of them. We needed the newbies, and we must keep all the current members. Losing more members might be catastrophic. The Lady Captain could not be seen as rude, even if she did have a list for half a dozen kinds of liquor in her pocket that needed to be taken care of immediately.

More questions about the food.

More comments about the pool, tennis courts, and the course.

After four conversations wherein I extolled CGC's many golfing virtues and another half an hour later, a group of ladies grabbed my elbow as I walked by, dragging me into their circle for a brief discussion.

I tried to dodge because the bar needed me to order the

booze, but two of the women latched onto my elbows. I smiled and desperately looked for a way to flee.

A dark-haired woman leaned in to kiss me on the cheek, but I didn't know who she was. Her head loomed large over the crowd as she swooped in for the greeting. *Holy heck,* but I could take a cheek-peck from a stranger for the club.

The woman's skin smelled like the club's green-and-forest balsam soap that we stocked in the ladies' locker room and the showers, a subject of some contention at the Ladies' League board meetings. Some people wanted something more flowery and feminine. Others liked the balsam because it really stripped off sweat and stink. The fresh scent was pleasant in the large room that was becoming the slightest bit stale from the mixed sweat of golfers covered up with perfume and aftershave.

The woman stepped back and said to me, "Bee, settle a question for us."

I almost jumped back from her. There were so many new guests I didn't know at the party, and it was weird to have one of them grab at me like that and know my name. She was wearing a slim, black formal dress with a silver embellishment at her bustline and opera-length white gloves. She was radically overdressed for an appetizer reception following a golf tournament, and her face was pink and free of make-up. From her crow's feet and forehead puckers, she looked a bit north of fifty.

The woman was standing with some club members,

though, including Pauline Damir. We'd ordered the flowers for tonight from Pauline's florist shop. From the way Pauline was listing to the side and grinning moistly, it looked like she'd had more than a few drinks.

The strange woman continued, "We think the club should have yoga classes in the clubhouse on a couple of weekday mornings. Don't you think that would be a value-added service that would attract new members?"

It took me a second of blinking to recognize the woman standing in front of me. I almost jumped in surprise that she was Ann Carmo, whom I'd known for years. Ann had worked as a kindergarten room aide for me back when we were young, before she'd had her kids and stayed home to raise them. Her kids were away in college or on their own, now. Ann was on half the club's committees because, when people asked for someone who would do a job or work on a project, Ann always stepped up. She was on even more committees and boards than I was.

"Oh, good gravy, Ann, I'm so used to seeing you on the golf course with your hair back in a ponytail and sunglasses and a hat on. I don't think I've ever seen your whole face with your hair down. You look great!" And she did, even though she wasn't wearing make-up, and I don't think I'd ever caught her without her bright red lipstick before. Her black, floor-length gown was fantastic, though.

Ann laughed loudly over the crowd's chatter, and her hand fluttered in the air. "Yes, well, I guess I over-dressed for the après-golf appetizer reception. Now, about my yoga idea?"

All that made sense. I said, "I'm not sure we should make a commitment like that because of the budget."

Ann's eyes widened, and her nose was above mine because she wore high heels, so I had to look up at her widening eyes. "Oh, we wouldn't have to spend any money. We could ask one of the local yoga instructors to do a class here and make it a ten- or twenty-dollar donation from the people who attend. That way, there is no additional expenditure on the club's part."

"That does sound good," I said. "We'll talk about it next week, okay?"

Ann beamed. "Next week. You bet."

When I finally got upstairs to my office to call about the booze, I flipped on the light and sat down at my desk, leaning back in my chair. As Lady Captain, I was entitled to a small office to organize the Ladies' League, events, and such.

Oliver Shwetz must have gone back down to the party after his few deep breaths. I'd see if I could find him later to check on him.

Just then, I needed to arrange for a booze delivery for the club.

In a big city, a service might have picked up the liquor and delivered it, but in a small town, connections are everything.

A Murder at the Country Club

I tapped my phone's screen, found a contact, and let it dial.

A man's gruff voice answered, "Hello? Mrs. Bee?"

I had taught Jacob Hibbert's four kids and a couple of his grandkids when they had been in kinder, and habits die hard. Mrs. Bee had been a perfect kindergarten-teacher name, and it had stuck after I'd retired. "Jacob, there's been a catastrophe over at Canterbury Golf Club. It seems that the bar has only one-quarter of a bottle of Glenmorangie Eighteen and even less of a few other staples. Is there any way I could entice you to bring us a case or two of your finest liquors?"

Jacob chuckled over the line. "You managed to get my grandson reading before you retired, something I thought would never happen. What do you need and how much, Mrs. Bee?"

I rattled off the list that the bartender, Maurice, had handed me. "Or any rational substitutions if you don't have something on hand."

Jacob hemmed and then said, "I hate to tell you this, but I'm going to have to ask for payment before we unload the boxes."

That was unusual. "The club has stellar credit. Have our checks bounced?"

"Not bounced, but that Ruddy Agani keeps putting off paying your liquor bill. We have a standing order for delivery every month, but your account is three months in arrears. That's why we didn't make the usual delivery last week. Didn't he tell you?"

No, Ruddy Agani had not mentioned that the club had not received its scheduled liquor delivery only days before an important prospective-member reception. Oh, I could just punch him sometimes.

Surely, the club's financial difficulties hadn't gotten so bad so fast that we hadn't been paying our bills. "Just a second, Jacob."

I logged onto the club's daily operating bank accounts through our computers. I had view-only access but didn't have the authority to cut and sign checks or authorize purchase orders.

Plenty of money was in the account designated for paying the bills.

I could imagine what Ruddy would say, though. He would ask why the club should have to pay for people to drink alcohol. He didn't drink alcohol. He didn't approve of drinking alcohol. Why should he have to pay for people who did?

And then, once again, I would remind Ruddy that the club did not give away the alcohol. We sold it in the bar area, and the club made a substantial profit from alcohol sales, which lowered all the members' dues, including his.

And then a few weeks later, we would do it again because Ruddy loved to find reasons to believe he was persecuted or somehow having to pay for other people's privileges, even though he was always wrong.

To Jacob, I said, "It's just reprehensible that a business would not pay its vendors, especially small business owners. I'll have a check in hand for tonight's delivery and the whole bill. Please tell me how much we owe you and how much these cases of liquor are, too."

Jacob said a number that was neither surprising nor exorbitant. As a matter of fact, it was quite reasonable. Overly so. Jacob must be giving us a break on the prices, which made Ruddy's failure to pay him all the more deplorable.

I said, "I'll meet you by the deliveries door with the check. Thank you for your patience with us, Jacob."

"That's okay, Mrs. Bee. See you in fifteen minutes."

We hung up, and I looked into the corners of the room, sighing. "Well, Henry, I'm trying. I don't know if we'll be able to save the club, not with nearly sixty families quitting within a month, but I'm trying. It's funny that I feel you more here than anywhere, but that's why I moved into a smaller place after you were gone. This is where I feel you the most, in the clubhouse and on the course. I still miss you, my Henry."

The office was silent, but even after a few years, I needed to talk to him sometimes.

I sat in my office for a few more minutes, listening to myself breathe, before I went to round up the caddies who were doing double-duty as waiters to ask them to carry the cases of booze into the bar once it arrived.

CHAPTER 4

ONCE I HAD the caddies lined up to carry in the liquor when it was delivered, I went to find Ruddy Agani to demand that he cut a check for Jacob.

Only a few people had the authority to cut and sign checks, including Ruddy Agani, the hothead who had stormed out of the clubhouse. Others included the treasurer of CGC, Erick Walters, and the club's manager. Ruddy was a financial officer on the Ways and Means committee.

Unfortunately, the club manager wasn't at the glow-ball tournament that night—something about his daughter's wedding—so I needed to find Ruddy. If Ruddy had already gone home, it might be easier and more pleasant to call one of the other two.

The dining room and entertaining rooms were both stuffed with people, but Ruddy was tall enough for his peppered, bristly head to be seen easily in the crowd. I stood on one of the lower stairs to look but didn't see him, so I asked around.

No one had seen him since he'd stormed out.

Ruddy wasn't in the bar, either, which wasn't surprising, considering his aggressively teetotaling opinions.

I asked my uncle Arnie if he could find out where Ruddy was.

Uncle Arnie meandered through the dining room with his drink for a few minutes, chatting, before he came back to me. "He's not inside. After Ruddy flounced out through the entertaining room's doors, he walked out onto the course. Someone said it looked like he was heading the wrong way down the eighteenth fairway. No one has seen him come back in."

"So, he's still out on the course?" I asked, looking out the windows into the black night. The Canterbury Golf Club was situated in the exurbs, far out in the land of small family farms, dairies, and a winery. The night out there was dark, and Ruddy had been gone for over an hour and a half.

One of the bag boys jogged up to me. "Mr. Agani's SUV is still in the parking lot. His clubs are in the back, a set of beat-up TaylorMades. I could see his bag tag, so it's definitely his vehicle. And I know his crappy clubs, too. I looked all around the parking lot, but I didn't see him out there, either."

I didn't like that Ruddy was out on the course, alone in the dark. "Okay. So, we need to take a walk to find Ruddy, if for no other reason than he needs to pay Jacob's Package

Store for the booze we've been drinking."

And we needed to check on him. Almost two hours is a long time to wander around on a dark golf course, even if he was having a rage fit.

I snagged Trudi to go with me because I knew she'd be glad for a break from the crowds.

Even though Ann Carmo was dressed in an evening gown, when I asked in her cluster of girls if someone wanted to go with us to check on Ruddy, Ann stepped up. Ann always stepped up when needed.

As we passed a group of guys, Ann snagged Erick Walters by the arm to go with us.

He grumbled but looked at his wrist. "Well, I need more steps, anyway."

Erick Walters was a big, strong guy who could drag one of us out of any quicksand that the course's chronic overwatering might cause, even though quicksand had never actually been spotted at CGC. Erick's wife, Afia, laughed as Ann dragged him off, exclaiming, "But you just came back!"

Trudi popped back into the ladies' locker room to change into her golf shoes before we walked the course, and Erick did the same in the gentlemen's locker area. I had taken my golf shoes home to clean them that day since I hadn't planned to play in the glow-ball tournament.

There were too many things to organize, and I'd acted as a starting marshal to get the foursomes out onto the course for the tournament. We'd set up three holes with the glow-ball equipment, and my job had been announcing the foursomes and shooing them into the dark.

I turned to Erick as we were preparing to walk outside. "Erick! You're the club treasurer! You can write a check for the liquor, right? Then we wouldn't have to go search the highlands for Ruddy in the middle of the faffing night? Please?"

Erick winced and squinted as he looked out the dark windows at the inky golf course. "I'm afraid not. There's a strict delineation of duties. One of the committee financial officers like Ruddy has to write the checks for incidental expenses. I only write the checks for monthly, recurring expenses like insurance, electricity, and water bills."

"Oh, jeez," I laughed. "The water bill."

He chuckled. "Tell me about it. I was on the board of the Gnostic Yacht Club before it closed down, where people hosed down their multimillion-dollar yachts every time they got some saltwater on them. I swear by all that's holy, they tried to fill up the ocean so their ships would float higher. But the water bill there was one-tenth of what we use here. When it's raining and yet Bhagwan Das has the sprinklers spraying the greens in the rain, I want to punch a wall."

I laughed. "Okay, let's go find Ruddy."

We all grabbed our jackets from the mudroom and headed out the back doors, past the patio, and down the fairway of the eighteenth.

Trudi's usual, enormous purse swung from her shoulder.

Ann bobbled along in her pumps, walking on her toes to avoid stabbing her high heels into the fairway.

As soon as we stepped off the patio, the wind picked up and blew my hair around my face. The glowing stripes that had lined the fairways and lit up the holes had faded to barely visible smears in the starry night.

We pulled out our cell phones and switched on the flashlight apps. Four beams of light sliced through the light fog and painted white circles on the black fairway and thick trees lining the sides of the golf course.

"Ruddy!" I called as we walked.

Ann, beside me, did the same, as did Erick beyond her.

The night was quiet as we walked, our shoes squelching on the tightly mown grass and thick loam underneath.

I groused, "Dew is soaking right through my shoes. I can't believe I am ruining a pair of loafers just to go find Ruddy because he stomped off."

Beyond Ann, Erick nodded. "I'm glad I changed into my golf shoes to walk out here. This grass is so wet that it's spongy."

On my other side, Trudi muttered, "Bhagwan Das probably watered it as soon the glow-ball tournament finished because our water bill isn't quite exorbitant enough this month."

Ann grumbled about her shoes, too, but kept up with the rest of us.

Light from our dancing flashlight beams cast our faces in

gray, and while we were near the clubhouse, some of the light and music from the party spilled through the windows and cast a ghostly aura over the eighteenth fairway.

As we trudged farther into the golf course, the light from the clubhouse faded away, leaving only the occasional flash from our cell phone beams to see each other.

"Ruddy?" I called out as we walked the wrong way down the eighteenth fairway, from the green to the tee box. "Hey, Ruddy! Where are you? We need you to write a check!"

I looked past Ann, watching Erick as he shined the flashlight randomly all over the course around us, at the bushes, the tops of the trees, and sometimes the sky. "I don't know where Ruddy could have gotten himself to."

To my left, Trudi's flashlight beam wiggled in the night. "Ruddy! Come on! Quit sulking and get back here!"

Trudi could be direct to a fault, but the world needed people like her. Right now, we needed Ruddy to get back to the clubhouse and do his job as a financial officer of the Ways and Means committee.

Or else we needed to get someone else to do it.

Walking on a pitch-black golf course in the middle of the night seemed like a great place to broach the delicate subject of restructuring the financial permissions of the club, so I said, "You know what, guys? We need to add more people who can write checks for the club. Jacob told me that Ruddy has not been paying vendors on time, and these vendors are our friends and neighbors here in Canterbury. We are not talking about doing business with big corporations. We are talking about Jacob Hibbert, our neighbor and friend who owns the local package store, and our club owes him three months' worth of bills. It pains me to say it because I don't like to criticize, but maybe this just isn't Ruddy's wheelhouse."

Erick said, "I've heard he does it in his own finances, too. He likes having the money in his accounts, no matter if he owes it to someone or not."

"These businesses might be charging us late fees, and we can't afford an extra ten percent or whatever just because Ruddy isn't paying the bills every month. Maybe we should have Ruddy doing other, less time-sensitive things for the club, and maybe somebody else should take over paying the bills."

Erick nodded. "Frank was just telling me the other day that the club hadn't paid the purchase orders for the grass seed from the home improvement store."

"Would Ruddy write the checks to them, too?"

"Yep. Any incidental or variable charge that would come out of the daily operating budget is his responsibility."

"This is exactly what I'm talking about," I said. "When Jacob told me that he hadn't been paid, I checked our accounts. The daily operating account has plenty of money. You guys know that we have a long-term financial problem, right?"

Ann nodded. "I've heard about the dues situation, but anyone could figure out that there is a problem when sixty-odd people are suddenly gone. Even Cintia joined up at Greens of Grass, and she hates riding in carts. You have to take a cart up there at Greens of Grass. I don't know why she would join up there."

To my other side, Trudi piped up, "Because with the discount they're offering, it's so much cheaper than Canterbury. I thought about joining up there for two years and then coming back."

"Oh, I hope you wouldn't do that." Losing Trudi as a golf partner would have been terrible. If she had quit the club and joined at Greens of Grass, I might have had to do the same.

That chain reaction was probably why we'd lost sixty memberships so fast.

"Eh," Trudi said. "Seemed like too much work to switch, but I would have taken you with me. I'm not joining some weird new club without you."

I bumped her with my shoulder, a quick buddy-hug while we were out on the golf course in the dark.

"Jeez." Ann swung her flashlight beam over the eighteenth tee box, the white light picking out the low bumps of the black, white, and red tee markers. "How far do you think Ruddy walked?"

Erick said, "If he was trying to walk off his temper tantrum, it could have been quite a way."

A Murder at the Country Club

I swung the beam from my phone across the space between the golf holes, looking for a man's dark shape among the trees. The shadows bent as I moved the flashlight. As far as I could see in the beam of my cell phone, the area was empty. "I don't know. Which way should we go?"

"I have no idea," Ann said, shaking her head. "Ruddy! Where are you?"

Erick flashed his light over the trees. "Let's just walk the course. At least we can say that we were methodical if we can't find him. Are any of the other financial officers here?"

"Not that I saw," Ann said.

Trudi strode out in the lead. "Right. Off to the seventeenth, then."

I said to Erick, leaning behind Ann to talk to him, "But, back to the problem of writing checks in the first place."

Erick shook his head. "Who would we nominate? We can't have too many people writing checks. It's not secure."

Ann shook her head, her hair swishing around her shoulders. "I think we should keep approval power and check-writing power separate, like it is now. It's kind of a check and balance, so to speak." She chuckled at her joke.

My flashlight beam swung through the dark, and the tiny reflectors set into the flagpole of the seventeenth hole sparkled in the night.

A long, dark hump lay on the green near the flagpole.

Trudi asked, "What's that?"

Ann asked, "Where?"

Erick squinted, which I could see in the glow from his cell phone screen. "Uh-oh. Is that—"

We started running.

Ann stumbled in her heels, and I caught her elbow as we ran.

Beside me, Trudi asked, "Is it him? Did he have a heart attack or something? Oh, we should have gone and looked for him sooner."

When we reached Ruddy, our hearts already pounding because we were golfers, not marathon runners, we aimed our cell phone beams at him. His head was turned where he lay on the ground, so we could see his face. His eyes were open, and his mouth gaped.

A gleaming knife, its blade slicked with something dark, lay on the ground beside him.

A long, black stain spread over the velvet grass.

Oh, no.

"Ruddy, are you all right?" I stepped forward, wanting to touch him to comfort him or something, but I didn't want to hurt him further if he were wounded. Jostling him might make him bleed more. I held my hands, fingers splayed, and felt suspended in the air.

Ann gasped, "What happened?"

Trudi scowled at Ann. "I think it's pretty obvious."

I asked, "Did he hurt himself? Was he that distraught over the argument with Oliver?"

Trudi pushed my hands down and shone her phone's

light over Ruddy. "It doesn't look like the blood is coming from his wrists, as would be common if he had tried to commit suicide. There's blood on his shirt, near his heart."

I saw the vermillion patch on his shirt, the only spot of color in the black and gray night. "Is he dead?"

Erick walked around the green, only glancing at Ruddy with his peripheral vision before bending to peer at the knife. "It's just a steak knife. How could a steak knife kill anyone?"

Erick extended his hand toward the knife, reaching like he might pick it up.

He did it so fast that his fingers were around the metal, his knuckles touching the ground, when Trudi yelled at him, "Don't touch the murder weapon!"

Erick jumped back, his hands open in front of his chest. "Jeez, I didn't think."

I said, "Maybe he's just hurt. Maybe he's not dead."

Ann said, "I'll call 911." Her cell phone flashlight was already off, and she was thumbing something on her phone. "Hello? There's been an accident or something. Ruddy Agani is lying on the seventeenth green at Canterbury Golf Club, and he's not moving." She covered the microphone of the phone with her other hand. "They're asking if he's alive."

Trudi glared at Ann. "He didn't sit up and say hi."

"We don't know," Ann told the dispatcher. She looked back up. "The ambulance is on the way. They're asking us to check and see if we can find a pulse or if he's breathing."

I craned my neck, bending and peering at Ruddy's open, unblinking, eerily still eyes.

Erick stepped backward, wincing.

"I can try to check." Ann kneeled beside him and hesitantly reached out to touch his arm. She wedged her phone between her ear and her shoulder and, wincing, pressed her fingers against his wrist. She frowned and grabbed his wrist more firmly, even rolling his arm as she tried, but she shook her head. "I don't feel anything."

Trudi sighed and walked closer to him. "Everyone expects the former scientist not to be squeamish about anything."

My BFF Trudi was small but made out of steel.

"You are a biologist," I commented, not meaning anything by it.

She crouched beside him and craned her head, inspecting him. She plucked blue, non-latex gloves out of her purse and stretched them over her hands. "I was a cell-biology neuroscience professor. I grew cells in flasks and streaked germs on gelatin, for the most part. I didn't dissect anything after undergrad. When a donor came in, one of the pathologists took care of them and passed the tissue samples on to me."

"But you'll do it?" I asked.

"Yeah. I'll do it." Trudi kneeled beside him, careful to avoid the darkened grass, and gingerly touched Ruddy's neck, feeling for a pulse, and then his chest. She frowned. "I don't feel a pulse. I don't think he's breathing, either."

Ann relayed the information and tapped her phone off. "They said they're on their way."

Trudi said, "I could dust that knife for fingerprints."

"You are not going to touch the murder weapon," I told her, horribly reconciling myself to the idea of murder and that Ruddy was gone. "I won't let you."

She bobbled her head. "Yeah, that's probably not a good idea, anyway."

The night seemed darker around us, like it could have hidden anyone or even a lot of people. I aimed my flashlight beam around the green at the trees and fairways, and I stepped closer to Trudi. "Do you think they're still around?"

Ann walked over to us, avoiding the stain and the knife. "That's scary."

Erick stood closer, too, and we waited until the police and paramedics arrived.

Lale Kollen, the reporter from the *Canterbury Tales,* rode out in the golf carts with them, practically giddy with excitement at her scoop.

The flash from Lale's camera lit the trees and fairways like lightning striking the clubhouse.

CHAPTER 5

THE NEXT MORNING, Saturday, Canterbury Golf Club was closed while the police investigated the crime scene on the seventeenth green.

Four police cruisers and one more car were the only ones in the empty parking lot when I pulled in, which was so odd for a weekend morning.

That week's Ladies' League needed overseeing, and scores needed to be tabulated and prizes assigned from the previous week, so I ended up working in my little office at Canterbury Golf Club while two Canterbury police officers and another man walked down the eighteenth fairway toward the scene of the murder.

Some people might have said that I shouldn't have been there because I was a witness to the murder after the fact, or at least because I found Ruddy's deceased body. However, when things needed doing, I didn't slack off just because the evening had been a little rough. Teachers know there are always papers to grade.

Even when I had been teaching kindergarten, there were always papers scrawled in toddlerish crayon handwriting to be corrected and have a star pasted on them.

Adding up all the scores from the scrawled handwriting on the score sheets and distributing stars and stickers in the form of pro shop credit was oddly similar to grading kindergarten papers.

Trudi had won low-net on Wednesday's match, which meant she got twenty dollars in pro shop credit for the week. I double-checked her score, just because I didn't want anybody to think I was cheating and giving the prize to my friend, but Trudi had won it. She had improved so much at golf over the past year.

I was blathering in my own head, trying to forget about seeing Ruddy's body lying on the seventeenth green.

Eventually, I couldn't take it anymore, and I pushed myself away from my desk to see if the police had found any additional evidence on the golf course.

Two officers were walking down the eighteenth as I strode up the fairway, and they nodded to me as we passed.

The morning was sunny and bright, though the stiff New England spring breeze still tugged at my clothes as I walked. As I marched up the eighteenth fairway onto the golf course, three figures stood in the bright sun near the seventeenth green. I recognized all three of them because Canterbury is a small town.

A Murder at the Country Club

The tall man standing on the left was Constable Sherwood Kane. In Canterbury, as in many New England towns, Town Constable was an elected position, not a professional position like the police chief. The town constable was often called out for investigations such as this. He represented the town's interests as well as justice, and as with most people, he was a friend of mine. "Hello, Sherwood."

He nodded at me and smiled, showing white teeth. "Good morning, Bee."

On the green, a dark stain still marred the grass that was shaved close to the ground. It seemed like an astonishing amount to come out of a wound caused by a mere steak knife.

The other two people standing on the green were two police officers from the Canterbury Police Department, meaning that ten percent of the town's police force was standing on the green at Canterbury Golf Club. The other eighteen officers must be hiding in the bushes somewhere, waiting to give traffic tickets to tourists for not coming to full and complete stops at intersections.

I nodded to the two officers, too. "Hello, Sandy and Gregor."

They both grinned and said in unison, "Hello, Mrs. Bee."

Yes, I had taught them both in kindergarten, and now they were police officers because children grow up too fast.

The body of Ruddy Agani had been taken to the local

hospital sometime during the night, probably while the police had been taking statements from Trudi, Ann, Erick, and me. We'd talked to the police for about an hour, racking our brains and trying to find any information that would help them. I didn't think I'd been successful at that.

Everybody knew that Ruddy had argued with Oliver earlier.

Several people had heard me offer him my office and seen him head in that direction.

Sherwood asked, "How are you today, Bee? Are you okay?"

"I'm doing okay, Sherwood. Thank you for asking."

Sherwood was a nice guy, tall and strong and ruggedly handsome. He was a year or two older than myself, so he certainly hadn't been one of my kindergarten students. Trudi had been after me to say yes when he asked me out for coffee one of these days, but I was still talking to my dead husband when no one was looking. I wasn't ready for coffee dates, even with a nice guy like Sherwood. I wasn't sure I'd ever be ready.

"Would you mind if we asked you a few questions, Mrs. Bee?" Sandy asked.

It made complete sense to me that Sandy had grown up to be a police officer. She'd always been sweet and helpful in kindergarten, but she made sure that no one threw sand in the sandbox and had found it very important to make sure that all of our lines were straight when we'd walked to the music room or library. "Sure, Officer Sandy."

Okay, that was weird. It was always weird to treat one of my former students like an adult after I had taught them to write their names and tied their soggy shoelaces.

Officer Sandy asked, "Were you at the party the whole night?"

I nodded. "The glow-ball tournament was my idea, and I organized the whole thing. It seemed like a really good idea to recruit new members, right up until we found Ruddy here on the seventeenth green."

"Were you in the clubhouse's dining room the whole time after Mr. Oliver Shwetz had that argument with Mr. Ruddy Agani?"

"The whole evening, yes, until we went out to find him. Needless to say, the evening took a downturn at that point."

Constable Sherwood's eyes crinkled a little at the corners, and he seemed to be repressing a smile. "Finding one of the guests murdered often puts a damper on a party, I've found."

"This is the first time I've found someone murdered at a party, so this is quite the new experience for me," I told him.

Maybe I shouldn't have been so flippant, considering what happened later, but Sherwood was biting his lip and seeming to have an even harder time refraining from smiling.

My other ex-student Gregor asked, "Other than Oliver Shwetz, who else did the victim have an altercation with that night?"

"No one that I know of. When I saw Ruddy and Oliver arguing, I went right over to break it up."

Sandy and Gregor sneaked a glance at each other and were trying not to smile.

"Is something funny?" I asked, conscious that I sounded exactly like the teacher I had been.

Sandy and Gregor stared at the grass for a minute, and finally, Gregor said, "No kid in your classroom dared start an argument. Whenever anyone said anything to someone else, you were right there, every time."

"Yes, well, anticipating arguments is a necessary job skill that kindergarten teachers often develop, along with eyes on the backs of our heads."

Gregor elbowed Sandy. "I told you that she had eyes on the back of her head."

Sandy laughed and asked, "So, with your eyes in the back of your head, did you see anything else at the party that we should know about?"

I smiled at my two ex-students, who were so cute while they were doing their little jobs. "I offered Oliver my office to cool down for a while after their altercation. He went directly to the stairs and went up to my Lady Captain's office on the second floor. His cardiologist had told him that stress was bad for his heart."

Sandy asked me, "So, you didn't leave the party?"

"I was so busy talking to prospective members, answering questions, and making sure everyone was having a good time that I wouldn't have had the chance to leave the clubhouse. I didn't notice if anyone was doing anything suspicious."

Sandy nodded, the sunlight shining off of her black police hat. "Yeah, you never saw the bad in anybody, anyway. I didn't think we'd get much out of you."

I wasn't sure whether to be complimented or insulted by that, so I chose to be complimented, probably because I didn't see the bad in anybody.

I wondered if that was true, and if it was, maybe that was why I was having problems suspecting that any of my friends might be capable of murdering Ruddy Agani.

Maybe I shouldn't be so quick to see the good in everyone. Maybe I should be a little more jaded.

Being a bit more suspicious might've saved Ruddy's life.

Officer Gregor held up a Ziploc bag holding the blood-encrusted knife. "Does this look familiar?"

I glanced at it, but I didn't like looking at a murder weapon very much. "It seems to be the knife that we found on the seventeenth green last night next to Ruddy Agani's body."

Officer Sandy asked, "Have you ever seen it before?"

"It's one of the steak knives from the club. Steak was served last night before the glow-ball golf tournament, so every place setting had a steak knife. There were at least eighty of them sitting on the tables last night."

Gregor sighed. "We were hoping that only some of the

people had steak and would have had a steak knife."

"We served steak and lobster. Everyone had a steak knife, and everyone had a nutcracker for the lobster."

"That wouldn't have narrowed it down anyway," Sandy said. "Even if only half of the people had had the steak and thus a steak knife, it doesn't mean that someone else couldn't have grabbed a dirty steak knife on their way out."

Gregor said, "I was hoping you could give us a place to start, Mrs. Bee. Do you know of anybody else who was mad at Mr. Agani?"

"From what I understand, quite a few people were mad at him."

Constable Sherwood and the two police officers groaned and looked around themselves in discomfort.

I continued, "Evidently, Ruddy Agani didn't like to pay his bills, even though he had the money. He didn't like to pay the club's bills either, even though we had the money, too. He also didn't like to pay his clients' bills."

Constable Sherwood ran his hand through his hair, messing up the black strands streaked with gray. "Can you get us a list of the people that the club owes money to?"

"Maybe, but I'm just on some of the committees. I think the treasurer of the club or one of the other financial officers are going to have to go through all of our accounts and figure out whom Ruddy had not paid. Erick Walters is our treasurer."

Sandy consulted her phone. "He's the man who was

with you last night when you discovered the body, right?"

"Oh, yes. Yes, he is."

Sandy shoved her phone in her hip pocket. "We've already talked to him once this morning. I guess we have to go back over there again this afternoon, Greg."

The two young police officers left, leaving me alone with Constable Sherwood. "The course looks like it's in really good shape," he said.

"Bhagwan Das has been working hard to get it in shape for all these membership drive events."

He frowned while staring at the short grass of the seventeenth green. "I thought the club went to spikeless golf shoes a few years ago."

I looked over at where Sherwood was looking at on the green. A constellation of tiny holes pinpricked the velvety short grass and sod beneath. "We did, but some people insist on wearing traditional spiked cleats. You can repair spike marks in your line now, you know, not just ball marks on the green."

"I cannot keep up with all these PGA rules changes."

"It's difficult. You haven't been out yet this year, have you?"

"There's been a lot going on. I'm up for reelection this fall, which means I have to do fundraising and campaigning again this summer."

"Have you thought about running for higher office? The town council could use good people like you. The school board needs conscientious people like yourself, too."

"I've thought about it. Maybe the next election cycle. Being the town constable leaves me plenty of time for golf," he said.

"Priorities are important."

"Walk you back to the clubhouse?"

I could tell Trudi that I had allowed Sherwood to walk me back to the clubhouse, and then maybe she would stop bothering me for a few minutes about going out to coffee with him. "Yes, I'm going back to the clubhouse."

We strolled down the eighteenth fairway, and the springtime sun warmed my shoulders.

Sherwood asked, "Are you fostering a kitten or a puppy right now?"

"A mama cat and her three newborn kittens," I said. "Someone dropped them off at the shelter just before she popped, and of course they didn't want the kittens around the other adoptable cats because they're too young to be vaccinated yet. They'll stay with me for another six or seven weeks."

"I still remember that herd of chinchillas that you fostered that one time," he said. "They were mischievous little things."

"But very soft. I still get pictures from the people who adopted them, mostly their little noses peeking out of shirts."

We reached the clubhouse, and I paused with my hand on the door. "See you around?"

"Yeah, I need to book the clubhouse for some of the fundraising events before the election this fall, but I'll see you around the golf course before that, I'm sure."

"I'll see you on the course, Sherwood."

CHAPTER 6

THE NEXT MORNING, Sunday, I was dressed and had checked on my foster kittens and a mama cat living in a good-sized box in my living room. The mama cat had a litter box in the little half-bathroom just steps away from the box, and food and water just outside her nursery. The kittens were still far too small to escape the box. I'd spent a delightful half-hour watching them drag themselves around the blanket in there, mewing blindly for the mama cat, who was chowing down on a special high-fat cat food for nursing mothers. I had a stack of cans near her area, and she was already not shy about letting me know when the food in her bowl had gotten low.

She wasn't shy with me at all anymore, and she butted my knee for pets before she climbed back into the box to nurse her babies. Mama cat was a ginger tiger with white feet, and her kittens were every permutation of orange, white, and black. They would go back to the town shelter for adoption when they were old enough, though the shelter and I had an understanding that if mama cat didn't find a home, she would come back and stay with me.

My mind circled around a name for her. Orlando, maybe, but I didn't call her that yet.

The shelter and I had had this understanding for several animals, but they had always found good and loving homes, which was better for me anyway. I organized golf trips for the club members, and I liked to travel to other places, too. Fostering animals was the perfect solution, giving desperate animals a loving, safe, temporary home until they found their forever homes and allowing me some pets to love and then send out in the world, happy, socialized, and healed of their trauma.

Just after I had stroked each of the kittens' tiny heads with one finger, beginning to socialize them so that they would grow up to be happy house cats, my doorbell rang a strident *bing-bong* through my small house, which I considered to be more of a cottage. I staggered up from the floor, and mama cat gave me one concerned meow before she hopped back in the box with her babies.

When I opened the door, I didn't bother to check through the peephole first, and maybe I should have.

Outside, standing on the winding path of brick pavers that led from the sidewalk to my front door, stood Coretta Dickinson, my next-door neighbor. She and her husband, Jim, were always angry at everything, and yet they argued with each other constantly because they always seem to be angry about the same things but for the wrong reasons. They were both known to call the police on their neighbors for any little thing, from the grass being too shaggy, to the trash bins being outside too long, to not liking the new paint on someone's window trim.

The neighborhood didn't actually have a homeowners' association, just one nosy, whiny homeowner.

The police officers who responded to the whiny complaints did discuss town appearance codes with the neighbors, but they nearly sprained their eyeballs as they did it. Everyone generally ignored Coretta and Jim Dickinson, but they lived directly next door to me.

"Hello, Coretta! I just made some lemon bars this morning. Would you like a lemon bar and some fresh coffee?"

Bribing them with baked goods resulted in fewer police calls for myself and the whole neighborhood.

Coretta carefully wiped her feet on the doormat outside the door, leaving barely damp tracks on the mat, and then on the mat inside the house before she walked inside. "Refined sugar is bad for one's teeth. You shouldn't eat so much of it."

Same old Coretta. "Maybe just a cup of coffee then? Or tea?"

"I've given up caffeine. Caffeine is bad for your health. It causes heart attacks and strokes and bad breath."

Yep, same. "If you'd like to sit down in the kitchen," I said, "I could get you a glass of water, with ice if you're living dangerously."

Coretta sniffed the air as if she smelled a bad odor. "I suppose I could have a glass of water."

She followed me to my small kitchen, decorated with blue and yellow lighthouses because I did love New England. At the café table inside, I set a tall glass of ice water for her, a cup of coffee for myself, and a plate of the lemon bars in the center.

Coretta sipped the ice water and eyed the lemon bars. "How did that golf-in-the-dark thing go Friday night?"

I sipped my coffee to give myself a moment to think.

Canterbury is a small town, and small towns have their grapevines. Coretta either already knew about the murder, or she would soon. Honestly, if she was the last person in town to know, it was only because people didn't talk to her because she was such a snitch about minor homeowner issues.

If I didn't tell her and she found out later, she would probably conclude that I was hiding something. If she thought I was hiding something, she would probably call the police and either insist that my lack of edging the grass around the pavers was indicative of a murderer's mindset, or else she would make something up, and then I would have to debunk whatever lies she told the police.

Really, the best option was probably to tell Coretta what

A Murder at the Country Club

I knew so that I didn't have to deal with anything worse. "We had a problem at the glow-ball golf tournament."

"Oh, no." Coretta grinned. "Was Friday the night that it rained, or did everybody just hate the idea?"

Trust Coretta Dickinson to come up with two snotty options. "No, it didn't rain, and everybody seemed to be having a great time. As a matter of fact, we sold out the event weeks ahead of time."

"Then, who did something to ruin it?"

Every time I let Coretta Dickinson into my house, I regretted it. "Maybe you can help me with this. Do you know anyone who was angry at Ruddy Agani?"

"I don't know who you're talking about."

"Rudolph Agani? The CPA who kept the books for several of the small businesses in town? I think he did the bookkeeping for Paul Hampdale's law firm and some of the knickknack stores and the ice cream shop down by the beach that the tourists go to."

"Never heard of him, but I don't gossip." Coretta took a lemon bar from the plate and bit into it.

"Well, of course, we would never gossip," I said, because otherwise, Coretta would tell everyone in town that I was a terrible gossip, "but I heard a lot of people were mad at him. I was just wondering if you knew anyone who was. He lived a few blocks away, over on Dorchester Street. His house has a low fence around it, and he has four beagles, if I remember right. His wife worked at the tee-shirt store during the tourist

57

season."

Coretta scrunched up her face as she chewed and thought. "I think I know the house that you're talking about. Those beagles barked every time I walked by on my daily walks. Someone should report him to the town for a noise violation."

"Someone murdered him last night at the golf club during the glow-ball tournament."

Coretta gasped, and crumbs fell from her lip onto the floor. "Right there in front of everybody?"

"No, he'd had a little argument at the reception, and then he walked out onto the golf course, I guess to blow off steam. We found him out there, already dead, two hours or so later. No one knows who did it."

"I never have approved of these country clubs serving alcohol to so many people at parties like that. Something like this was bound to happen. They should have known better."

"We've been holding two or more events at the club every month for thirty years. This is the first time anyone has been murdered."

"Still, this is what happens when people drink alcohol. They shouldn't do that, and country clubs shouldn't encourage it. I don't know why the town even allows a country club. We shouldn't have places where regular people are excluded."

"Pretty much anybody can join the Canterbury Golf Club. I don't think we've turned down a membership in thirty or forty years, and we wouldn't refuse anybody membership right now."

Coretta took another lemon bar. "Having places like that isn't good for the town."

"You're certainly entitled to your opinion." I'd used that phrase a lot with parents when I was teaching kindergarten.

"Once news of this murder gets around town, nobody's going to want to belong to such a country club anyway. I imagine that lots of people will quit, and certainly no one new is going to want to join up. I certainly wouldn't want to join a country club where a murder had occurred. I wouldn't ever feel safe there."

As much as Coretta was a whiny snitch, she had a point.

Once word got around town that Ruddy Agani had been murdered at Canterbury Golf Club, people might be afraid to join.

Coretta said, "That country club might have to close down like the yacht club did last year."

Oh, yeah. There was that, too.

I needed to get down to the club and work on damage control.

I stood. "Coretta, unfortunately, I have some places to go. I'll see you later."

Coretta took several more of my lemon bars from the plate. "I'll just take a few of these for Jim."

When I opened my front door to usher Coretta out of my house so I could leave, the *Canterbury Tales* newspaper lay on the front step.

MURDER AT THE COUNTRY CLUB, screamed the headline.

Dang. Everyone in town would know that Ruddy had been killed at CGC now.

CHAPTER 7

THE MORNING SUN bore down on the asphalt and the hood of my tiny car as I pulled into the Canterbury Golf Club. The parking lot was about a quarter full, and I recognized most of the cars that belonged to members and friends.

Over at the driving range, Constable Sherwood Kane's small SUV shone in the sunlight, and Sherwood's tall form swung a long club on the practice mats.

Just the man I wanted to see.

Hiking over to the driving range took just a few minutes, and I huffed as I trudged up the steep slope to where Sherwood stood, swinging his golf club in a wide, round arc. His ball flew down the range's fairway, a solid shot.

"You don't seem to have lost your swing this winter," I remarked.

Sherwood turned and, seeing me, grinned. "Hey, I didn't expect to see you here."

"Why wouldn't I be here? There's always something to

attend to. Ladies' League always needs new ranking sheets made."

"Did you see the newspaper this morning?" he asked.

"Oh, that. It doesn't concern me in the slightest." I felt bad about lying to law enforcement, but this was an extenuating circumstance. "I'm sure they'll find out who did it soon, and everything will go back to normal."

Sherwood shrugged and turned back to the fairway to hit another ball. "We sent the knife to the state forensics lab, but they're backed up. I'm not sure how long it'll take to get even the most basic fingerprint analysis on the knife. Might take months."

"Oh, I hope you're not going to let it drag out like that. People are going to be scared away from Canterbury Golf Club." I realized how bad that sounded. "And Ruddy's poor wife and family. They need some closure. They need justice. The police have to find the murderer so that his family and wife will have justice."

I didn't like myself very much at that moment.

Sherwood said, "Well, we can't do anything until we get the forensics back. Even if we did identify suspects, that all might be out the window if we get a fingerprint match for somebody else on the knife. It's a waste of police resources and town money to go chasing after suspects when one fingerprint might solve the case."

I sighed. "The steak knife was from the club. They go missing all the time. The serving staff thinks we must have magpies or elves that steal them. Even if the lab did find a fingerprint on the knife, it's possible that the murderer took someone else's knife."

Sherwood glanced at me. "Are you worried about your prints showing up on the knife?"

"No. I had the lobster. I didn't touch my knife. Surely, though, we can spare some officers to investigate who killed Ruddy. The Town of Canterbury employs twenty police officers, which is probably fifteen too many. Most of them end up sitting on the beach during the summer, giving out tickets to the tourists for littering. We only need a few officers to direct traffic when we get a traffic jam during Memorial and Labor Day weekends or to ask around when someone shoplifts a seashell picture frame from the knickknack shop. It's even still early in the season. The tourists don't even really arrive until after Memorial Day. I would hesitate to say that our finest are just sitting around drinking coffee and eating doughnuts, but when I was driving to the course this morning, I saw four police cruisers parked at Bess Eaton." That was the local doughnut shop. "What do they have to do that's more important than investigating the murder of a Canterbury citizen?"

"It's standard operating procedure to pause investigations when there is forensic evidence until the analysis comes back from the state forensics laboratory. I don't make the rules, Bee. I just make sure that the town is in compliance with them."

"So, it might be months before anyone even asks where people were when Ruddy was killed?" My voice rose in what I hoped was not hysteria, but it probably was.

Sherwood rubbed his chin. "I hope it won't be months. At the most, maybe three months."

"But," I stammered, "but Ruddy's family, and his wife, and justice."

"Bee, do you have information that I should know about?"

"No, I don't know anything! I don't know anything at all, and nobody else knows anything either. There's a murderer running around Canterbury, and it creeps me out. They might be a member of the club. They might be walking along the beach when I'm there next time. They might be standing behind me in the grocery store."

Sherwood cocked his head to the side and gave me a lopsided smile. "Most murders are personal. Chances are that this was an argument that got out of control. We've got someone watching Oliver Shwetz, so he's not going to argue with anybody else and then kill them."

"Do you think it was Oliver?" I asked him. "Should we revoke his club membership?"

"Due to my elected position in the town, I have no opinion about who it might or might not have been. My only concern is for the town and to make sure that the rules are followed so that the town's legal liability remains as limited as possible," Sherwood said while nodding vigorously.

So, Sherwood *did* think Oliver had killed Ruddy.

Okay, I had to figure out what the club should do about that.

Sherwood asked, "I'm going to ask you one more time because it feels like you're trying to tell me something. Do you know of anyone else who might have killed Ruddy Agani?"

"I just know that Ruddy was delaying payments from the club to a lot of local small business owners."

"Yes, you were supposed to get me a list."

"And I will, just as soon as I figure out how. I don't know if he was doing the same for his accounting clients. He might have been. Plus, he was just so unpleasant to everyone, so I don't think we should rule out anyone in his personal life."

Sherwood raised his eyebrows. "It sounds like you've thought about this a lot."

"Of course, I have. It concerns the club. I'm the Lady Captain here, and everything that concerns the club concerns me. Plus, Oliver wasn't accounted for after his argument with Ruddy. After the argument, I told him that he could go up to my office to cool down because his cardiologist had told him that getting upset wasn't good for his blood pressure, and then when I went up there later to make a phone call, he wasn't there. I don't know where he was during that time."

Sherwood frowned and rested his elbow on the top of his bag. "You went back to your office during the party last night, while Ruddy was missing?"

"Yes, I called Jacob Hibbert from up there because the bar was running out of liquor because Ruddy hadn't paid our bill at Jacob's package store for the past three months. I had to arrange with Jacob to have him deliver a case of scotch and a few other things to the bar, or else the bar was going to run out of alcohol during this very important reception. That's why I had to find Ruddy afterward, to get him to cut a check for Jacob."

"I thought Oliver Shwetz was in your office."

I thought about it for a minute. "He wasn't up there when I opened my door. He must have left before that."

Sherwood was still frowning at me. "Did anybody see you go upstairs? Did anybody see you come back downstairs?"

"I talked to Jason Hibbert on my cell phone. That would have a timestamp, and his cell phone would, too."

"But that doesn't establish your location when you made the phone call like a landline does. How long were you upstairs?"

"I don't know. Maybe twenty minutes? Maybe longer, because then I looked over the accounts to make sure that we had enough money in the daily operating account to pay Jacob what we owed him."

Sherwood was staring directly at me. "How much longer?"

I blinked in the strong sunlight. "I'm not sure. I know

that Ruddy was gone for almost two hours before we started looking for him, but I was mingling for most of that."

Sherwood took out his cell phone and tapped the screen a few times. "You didn't tell the police officers you had left the party and were unaccounted for, while the victim was still missing."

"I was rattled when I talked to them. I'd just found a dead body. I'm surprised I wasn't in the bar, sucking down half of Jacob's delivery."

"You didn't mention it to the officers yesterday morning, either," Sherwood said. "We're going to need you to talk to the police officers and amend your story, and you should make sure to tell us if anyone can corroborate when you went upstairs and when you came back downstairs, and especially if there's any evidence that you were in your office that whole time. There is a set of stairs that leads from the back of the second story of the clubhouse and right out down to that side door by the pro shop. In theory, and I'm not saying this happened, you could've come down those stairs while you were talking on the phone, gone and found Ruddy, killed him, gone back up the stairs to your office, and then back down the main staircase to the party. It's very possible that no one might've seen you leave the clubhouse."

"Well, you could say the same thing about Oliver Shwetz."

"Yes, we could. I need to add the possibility that Oliver went down those back stairs and out to the course to your statements, too."

And, I'd just made Oliver's life harder, which I had not meant to do, doggonit. "But you just said I must have been yammering on my cell phone the whole time. Someone would have noticed that."

"It was a loud party, from what the neighbors said. We had one noise complaint about the DJ. Even if you were talking, people might not have heard anything."

"And Oliver and I were both wearing light-colored shirts that night. He wore a white shirt, and I was wearing pale blue. I can't even properly cut up a steak without dripping the juice on myself. Someone would have noticed blood on our clothes if either one of us had stabbed a person with a knife. You saw all that blood on the green. Wouldn't I have gotten some of that on me in a—" I struggled to remember the correct terminology from all those forensic television shows. "—blood spatter or spray?"

"Not necessarily," Sherwood said. "When people are stabbed, they don't spray blood like a popping water balloon or a high-pressure pipe with a leak. Sometimes, they just drip a little."

"You saw the blood on the green. There was so much of it."

"It was a blood pool," Sherwood said, "that had sunk into the ground. Most of that could have seeped out of him, rather than sprayed out like a firehose that got loose."

There had to be a reason why I couldn't be a suspect. "I

wasn't gone that long when I popped up to my office."

But I had been. I'd been sitting in my office, talking first to Jacob and then to my dead husband for probably twenty minutes before I'd felt fortified enough to go downstairs to find Ruddy.

Sherwood said, "Well, we are going to have to establish a timeline for you, just to make sure."

"I thought you said you weren't going to investigate the murder at all because the forensic evidence isn't back from the state lab."

"Unfortunately, between you and Oliver Shwetz, we now have two suspects who were unaccounted for when the murder might've taken place. Other than investigating you and Oliver Shwetz, the police probably won't look any further for suspects until the forensic analysis is complete."

Great.

Just great.

I managed to make myself a suspect in Ruddy's murder and to make sure that the investigation was stalled.

That meant the murderer was going to be freely walking around Canterbury Golf Club, which likely would make people afraid to join the club.

And I didn't like the idea much, either.

How had I managed to make things worse?

Chapter 8

Inside the Canterbury Golf Club clubhouse, the air-conditioning blew at full blast because it was finally warm that day after being so cold for weeks, even during our nighttime glow-ball tournament just days before. The large, plate-glass windows of the clubhouse created a greenhouse effect, which helped with heating costs during the long, New England winter, but people don't golf much during the winter. The club needed to add some shades above those windows, but committing to that kind of expense right now would be foolhardy.

Up in my office, I opened my computer and stared at the screen, angry for allowing myself to become a suspect in something that I obviously hadn't done, which therefore impeded the investigation and delayed finding the real murderer. It was ridiculous. I was ridiculous. I shouldn't have said anything.

I resolved to keep my mouth shut and not discuss the

murder with anyone, for any reason, until the police had caught the real murderer. Canterbury Golf Club depended on me not to make this worse.

On the screen of my computer, the club's daily operating budget account was still open. I scanned the list of vendors, but they all seemed like perfectly reasonable businesses for a golf club to pay for services or goods. The names all seemed to be normal business names, even if I didn't recognize some of them.

Shoreline Landscaping, Inc.

Surf and Turf Meat Shop, which was a good butcher shop. I bought meat from them when I had company over.

DeWitt's Flower Nursery. They had nice mums last year.

Healthy Plant Organic Farm.

Handy Hands Carpet and Upholstery Cleaners. Good, the carpeting in the dining room was getting grungy.

I scanned the list, looking for anything unusual or weird, but even in a small town like Canterbury, I didn't know every vendor that might supply the golf club. Besides, there were a dozen other small towns near enough to have places of business that Canterbury might be using as vendors, not to mention some of the smaller cities located within an hour or two away.

A knock rattled my open office door.

When I looked up, Linda Agani, the wife of the deceased Ruddy Agani, leaned against the frame in my doorway, wearing golfing attire and a serious expression on her face. "I heard you found Ruddy after it happened."

I closed my computer and folded my hands on top of it. "I'm so sorry."

She walked in and sat in the chair in front of my desk. Her eyes weren't red, but she seemed quieter and more solemn than usual, and her sigh was heavy. "I still can't believe it."

"Me, either." I wasn't lying. It seemed unbelievable that someone, anyone, whom I knew had been murdered.

"The police won't tell me anything," she said.

"I don't think they know very much. I just talked to Constable Sherwood Kane, and he said that the police wouldn't even begin an in-depth investigation until after they get the knife back from the state's forensic lab to see if there are any fingerprints on it."

"Oh, no. That means it's going to be months before I can move."

"I told Constable Sherwood that the investigation should start now because Ruddy's family would want closure and justice."

"It's not just that. I'm moving to California."

"Permanently?"

"California seems like a good place to start over. I need to start fresh."

"This seems sudden. Maybe you should think about it for a couple of weeks, just in case maybe you don't want to move to California. Maybe you'll want to move to Arizona."

"I rented an apartment out there last week. It'll be ready for me to move in on the first of the month."

Last week? "But what about your club membership?"

"Didn't Ruddy resign the family membership and change it to an individual membership? He was supposed to."

I opened the computer on the desk between us and pulled up a spreadsheet that showed membership details.

Five more families were resigning their memberships effective at the beginning of the next month. The rival country club Greens of Grass had probably poached them with their loss-leader promotion, too, which meant I had even more memberships to make up for. When I flipped to the page for current membership changes, neither of the two entries were the Agani family. "No, he didn't submit a change. Do you want me to mark you down to change your membership status?"

Linda sighed another sad and heavy sigh. "I suppose you should since I'm moving to California and Ruddy isn't going to be around to play golf anymore."

"Am I missing something here?" I asked.

"You knew about the divorce, right?"

I leaned back in my chair, shocked. "No. I suppose I only saw Ruddy in committee meetings, and we tried not to talk about personal stuff in meetings. You know how there's always so much business to take care of. If he had mentioned it, I didn't hear him. I haven't seen you around the club much this year because you didn't sign up for Ladies' League this year. I'm so sorry to hear that."

Linda sadly contemplated her hands, knotted in her lap. "I've been unhappy for years. Our last kid went off to college last fall, and I stayed through the winter, hoping we could work things out or that things would get better. They didn't. I don't want to talk about him right now because I just wanted to get away from him and start a new life, but I never wanted this to happen to him." She paused, frowning, and a tear splashed on her hands before she repeated, "I would never have wanted something like this to happen to him."

"So, that's why you didn't come to the glow-ball tournament with him? Because you were planning on leaving soon, anyway?"

Linda shook her head, her dark hair swishing about her face.

Her hair was darker, with no gray streaks like she'd had last year during Ladies' League. She'd started coloring her hair.

Not that coloring your hair means you're a murderer. Half the ladies at the club would be indicted for murder if that were the case, including me. But maybe it did indicate that Linda had been thinking about starting a new life.

She said, "We had a fight that night. The last thing I said to him was, 'If that's how you feel, then maybe I should leave right now.' And I did. I walked out of the house, got in my car, and left. I figured he was going to go to the club for the tournament because we'd already paid for the tickets, and the tickets included dinner. Lord knows Ruddy wouldn't have wasted money that had already been spent just to chase his crying wife around. I wish I hadn't said that, though."

I said, "I'm so sorry."

Linda shrugged. "I've said a lot of things like that in the last year. We both knew that our marriage was ending. I hate to say it, but I'm relieved there isn't going to be a big divorce battle in court. Ruddy would have fought for every penny, and then no matter what I did get out of it to start my new life after raising four kids for thirty years, he probably wouldn't have written me a check until I'd threatened to have him arrested."

She sounded a little bitter, but anyone on the verge of divorce probably would.

And everyone else had been saying that Ruddy didn't pay his bills, too.

Linda placed her hands on her knees and pushed herself to her feet. "So, who do I have to tell that we're going to be resigning our membership, I guess, at the end of the month?"

I started typing her name into the next line on the spreadsheet. "I can do that for you right now. You don't need to go anywhere else."

"Thanks, Beatrice. I appreciate it. I'll be around a little bit over the next week or so. I've got to improve my golf game before I get to California. Year-round golf, you know?"

"Good luck, Linda. I'm so sorry about everything that

happened."

Linda's glance felt like a knife pointed in my direction. "How did you happen to find him?"

"I went looking for him to cut a check to Jacob Hibbert for a shipment of liquor for the bar. It seems that he'd been delaying payment to the club's vendors, and Jacob threatened to cut us off if we didn't pay him."

Linda closed her eyes, and they crinkled at the corners. "Yeah, I can see him doing that."

Linda walked out of my office, and I heard her footsteps on the back stairs as Trudi popped around the corner of my doorframe.

Trudi's blue eyes were wide as she whispered, "Did you hear that?"

I finished typing the Aganis' names and membership number into the spreadsheet so that Linda wouldn't be billed for club dues for next month. "Hear what? That she was divorcing him? I can't say I'm surprised. If he was half as awful to her as he was to everybody else, the only surprise is that she stayed with him this long."

"No, I meant that she didn't have an alibi for when Ruddy was murdered, and she knew where he was going to be."

I looked at Trudi over the top of my reading glasses. "Linda hardly seems the type to murder someone."

"You know as much as I do that anyone can snap. Anyone can get fed up, have enough of someone else's baloney, and just snap."

Trudi wasn't wrong. There were times when I yelled at my Henry and he yelled back at me, even though I would have never dreamed of doing something violent.

Maybe other people went a few steps farther.

That wasn't impossible to believe.

Trudi said, "And Linda is a club member. She could've taken one of our steak knives to kill him any time when they had supper at the club."

"Whoever killed him probably took a steak knife from dinner that night. Linda didn't come to the dinner or the glow-ball tournament. Indeed, I kind of noticed that Ruddy arrived without her and hoped he wouldn't want his money back for her ticket. If it was Linda, and I'm not saying it was, she would've had to have planned it so far in advance that she stole a steak knife from the club at some previous date."

Trudi flopped herself in the chair on the other side of my desk and stretched her short legs as far as she was able to. "Well, when was the last time they had dinner at the club? We can check their monthly bill and see when that was."

"They didn't eat dinner at the club that much. I'll bet Ruddy thought it was too expensive, even though it is cheaper than a lot of the restaurants around here." I clicked around on my computer and pulled up the Aganis' tab from the last month. "The only suppers on here are single meals after the men have their league, so that was probably Ruddy but not Linda. She hasn't eaten here this month, at all."

Trudi scowled. "That doesn't mean that she didn't walk into the club, where no one would have been surprised to see her at a tournament that she had bought a ticket to, and snag a steak knife earlier that night."

Trudi was not going to let go of this until I agreed that it was possible. "I suppose it could have happened that way."

"You should have let me dust that knife for fingerprints when we found it."

"We would've had a hard time explaining to the police why there was baby powder on the murder weapon."

Trudi shrugged. "We could have figured something out to tell them."

"Yeah, I talked to Constable Sherwood a little while ago, and he said they probably weren't going to do much of anything until they got the forensic analysis back from the state laboratory, and that could take three months or longer."

"That's awful. Oliver Shwetz will be walking around the club the whole time, leering at everybody and making them feel uncomfortable."

"Unfortunately, Constable Sherwood doesn't think he's the only suspect. I managed to sort of implicate myself when I was talking to him on the range earlier today."

Trudi glanced up at me and grabbed the arm of her chair. "Don't tell me anything, but if we need to figure out an alibi for you, I should know that I have to do that."

"Trudi, I didn't kill Ruddy!"

"I'm not saying you did, but if there's something that we need to explain, I should know it. You know I've got your back."

I must admit that it is comforting to have a friend who says that she will cover for you, even though she thinks you may have committed murder. "I didn't kill him, but I kind of don't have an alibi for part of the time when he might have been murdered."

Trudi pulled her phone out of her pocket and stuck it under her thigh, sitting on it. "Close your computer and put it away. Put your phone someplace where it can't listen to us."

Her paranoia was so sweet, if a bit misplaced.

"Trudi, I swear on a stack of Bibles, I did not kill Ruddy. I did not hurt Ruddy. I did not go out onto the golf course that night before we walked out there together. I was running around the clubhouse, organizing the event."

Trudi squinted at me, laid her phone on my desk, and then announced, "All right! I believe you! I believe that you were in the clubhouse the entire time, and you did not leave the clubhouse before the four of us went out and found Ruddy together! You were never alone at any point, and thus you have an alibi for the entire night of the glow-ball tournament!"

I touched the side of my head where a headache was forming. "Now that we've gotten that over with, I really didn't kill him. I'm really worried about the effect that an unsolved murder could have on the club, especially after that newspaper article this morning. It looks like Oliver Shwetz may be a suspect because of that argument they had right before Ruddy stomped out, and now it looks like the wife, Linda, may not have an alibi, even though I would be shocked if she had anything to do with it."

Trudi shook her head. "We need to find some solid, forensic evidence that will tell us who killed him."

"Or we could quietly and discreetly ask a few questions and see if we can rule out somebody like Linda so she can have closure and go on with her life."

Trudi frowned. "And make sure that the police don't suspect you. I don't like the thought of the police suspecting you at all. We need to find out who did this."

CHAPTER 9

STANDING IN FRONT of the women golfers enrolled in Ladies' League the next Wednesday morning was more nerve-racking than many things I've done in my life.

I never misplaced a kindergartner while I was on a field trip, but the flutters in my tummy and the shakiness of my fingers felt a lot like that one time when I had to step in front of a large father who was going to take out his anger on his kid. The brilliant sunshine warmed the top of my head, though the breeze chilled my ears.

The sheet of paper in my hands trembled, and I read the words as I held the microphone, "Today, Ladies' League is a shotgun start."

Snickering swept over the assembled group of women standing on the back of the practice putting green. Some of them held one of their hands over their mouths when I said the word "shotgun," but a few of them outright laughed in a mean way.

To be fair, a lot of them didn't.

I've known these women for years, and yet with just one murder accusation, they were turning on me.

Maybe I would be wary of someone who'd been accused of murder, too, but I wouldn't laugh at them.

If anything, laughing at a possible murderer seemed unwise.

They should take that to heart.

"Something funny?" I asked, and my voice boomed through the microphone and out the speakers hanging under the porch roof of the clubhouse.

They quieted down. I could tell that a lot of them lost interest with just that little bit of pushback, but some of the women—the ones who I knew were a little meaner than the others to begin with—were still giving me the side-eye.

Teachers know what to do when the mob is acting unruly. I fixed all of them with a strict gaze, standing above them with a stern look on my face and the thought in my head: *I see you, you little hooligans.*

It worked on kindergartners.

A few more of them quieted down, but there were still a half-dozen women whose glares were making me uncomfortable.

Nobody said being Lady Captain was easy, especially when one had recently been accused of murdering somebody.

I announced, "All threesomes should be at their starting

tee box at nine o'clock. I will blow the air horn, and that will be your signal for the first person in your threesome to tee off. You may decide amongst yourselves who has the honor. The groups will tee off at nine o'clock, sharp."

A woman's voice from the crowd said, "Sharp, like a knife?"

I couldn't answer anymore. I'd been the Lady Captain for five years. I'd put in a whole lot of volunteer work for the Canterbury Golf Club on numerous committees, and it seemed ridiculous that an unsubstantiated rumor was making these people say such unkind things.

Resolving to ignore the comment, I folded my notepaper into crisp squares and leaned downed to tuck it into my golf bag beside my current favorite golf ball, which looked like a yellow-and-black soccer ball.

A pair of scarlet golf shoes appeared in my peripheral vision.

I glanced up, finding Ann Carmo standing beside me. This time, I recognized her right off with her scarlet lipstick, wide sunglasses, and dark visor shading her eyes and even around to her ears. She was wearing new red Adidas golf shoes that matched her lipstick.

Ann announced in a loud voice, "Do you have something you want to say out loud, *Nell?*"

Nell?

Nell Rinaldi had belonged to the club for years. We'd served on probably five committees together, and she was saying stuff like that about me in front of everyone? I straightened and looked out over the group of several dozen women standing in the warm, springtime sunlight. Some ladies stood on the emerald, velvet practice green beside us, though most of the women stood on the asphalt-paved cart path, leaning on their pushcarts or sitting in their riding carts. Most of them were looking at their shoes or shifting from side to side, profoundly uncomfortable with the turn this morning had taken, but a few of the ladies were watching Nell and Ann closely.

Nell said, "Everyone who reads mystery novels knows that the person who found the body is often the murderer. Beatrice found the body, so there is a very likely chance that she murdered Ruddy Agani. I think the publicity of the murder is hurting the club, and I think Beatrice should step down as Lady Captain until this is taken care of."

"You're an idiot, Nell," Ann told her, struggling to stuff her hand into an old golf glove. The glove's fingers were gnarled with sweat and dirt, and Ann yanked the leather over her palm.

Under most other circumstances, if Ann had told one of our members that they were an idiot, I might've said something.

Not today.

Nell muttered, though everyone could plainly hear her, "Hey, I'm not the one who lost a glowing ball in the dark and got left behind."

That was weird. I hadn't even played in the glow-ball tournament.

Ann continued, "Beatrice obviously didn't kill Ruddy. Ruddy Agani was a huge, strong man. Even though Bee is obviously in great shape for a woman her age—"

Now, I was thinking about stopping her.

She dropped a tee and bent to pick it up. "—no one her size and age could possibly kill a man Ruddy's size. A man must have done it, like Oliver Shwetz. We all saw them arguing. It's obvious, right?" She winked at the crowd.

I wasn't sure Ann was right, but I didn't want to protest that I could easily be a murderer in front of everyone. I didn't like that she was blaming Oliver, though. He hadn't even been charged, let alone convicted.

Ann continued, "Especially since Bee is a little overweight and out of shape—"

I was going to have to stop her soon for my own peace of mind.

"—not to mention getting up there in years—"

That was over the line. I golfed almost every day, and I walked our hilly course with my clubs in a pushcart. I could easily kill someone, if I wanted to.

Not that I should announce that to the entire Ladies' League.

"—Not that Bee is morbidly obese or anything, but she's just packing a few extra pounds on her." Ann slapped her own slightly chubby behind. "I mean, we're all carrying a few extra pounds, am I right? Wilber tells me I need to diet every day."

I was done. "Ann, thank you for that spirited defense, but I think I'm okay now." I was holding onto a little bit of winter fluff, but that was no one's business but my own. Not to mention that I didn't tolerate anybody fat-shaming another person for any reason. It was uncouth and unkind, and I hadn't put up with such cruelty from my kindergartners, either.

Ann continued, "Just because Bee said that we should go look for Ruddy and it was her idea to look for him on the golf course, it doesn't mean that she had anything to do with it."

If Ann defended me much longer, I was going to end up in the electric chair. "Will you look at the time! We need to start making our way to the tee boxes right now."

"Yeah, we'd better go," someone else said. "We wouldn't want Bee to get mad at us."

Trudi stepped beside me and lifted her chin.

I laid my hand on her arm. My pride could not take any more defending that day.

Trudi announced, "Beatrice is one of the most dedicated members of this club. I happen to know that Greens of Grass Country Club offered her an entirely free membership to come and be their Lady Captain."

"Trudi," I whispered. That was supposed to be a secret.

"But she didn't take the free golf because she is loyal to

Canterbury, and she is loyal to you. You should all be ashamed of yourselves if you would even think that about Bee. Bee is one of the nicest, sweetest women I know, and if a roomful of thirty kindergartners didn't make her snap, nothing will."

"Oh, no," I said. "They were sweet. I loved my—"

"Rainy day schedule," Trudi said to me.

Well, okay.

"I don't think anybody should be accusing anyone else of murdering Ruddy Agani, anyway," Pauline Damir said to the assembled women golfers. "A lot of people were mad at Ruddy. His CPA firm did the bookkeeping for quite a few small businesses in town, like the Banks Funeral Home. I have a florist business, and the funeral home ordered a lot of flowers from me. They authorized the payments, but Ruddy Agani never paid their account unless I called and yelled at him. The last time I yelled at him, he still didn't pay. I have to pay the flower wholesalers when I order the flowers, so if someone doesn't pay me, I'm in debt."

Ann Campo said, "Yes, I heard that he did that a lot."

Pauline continued, "When someone else took over his accounts at his firm, the first thing I did was call them and get my money. I finally got a check this morning for the last six months' worth of flowers. I hate to say that I'm glad he's dead, but if something hadn't happened, my flower shop would have gone bankrupt, just because he wouldn't pay his clients' bills on time. Before this happened, I was looking into hiring Oliver Shwetz or some other lawyer to send Ruddy official legal letters or take him to small claims court. You know that, Ann."

Great, Pauline had just given herself motive, and I remembered that she had been at the glow-ball golf tournament that night. First, Ruddy had nearly barreled into her as he'd stomped out, so she had known where he had gone, and then she'd been standing with Ann quite a bit later and looking a mite wasted.

Anybody could fake being tipsy, though.

Or maybe she'd needed a stiff drink or three after what she'd done.

Suspecting my friends of murder was an awful feeling.

I asked Pauline, "Do you know of other people who had a problem with Ruddy not paying them from his CPA business?"

"Lots of people! If you get a list of his clients, you'll have a suspect list a mile long," Pauline said.

It seemed like everybody had wanted to kill Ruddy Agani, and yet everybody at Ladies' League was still looking at me.

"And on that note," I shouted over the crowd of women waiting for Ladies' League to begin, "you have ten minutes to get to your tee boxes before I will sound the air horn, and somebody from your group should tee off. Let's make sure everybody's in position so that everyone is safe. Ladies, let's walk out."

A Murder at the Country Club

Trudi turned to Ann Carmo. "Way to go with the backhanded defense there, Ann. I don't think 'Bee is too fat to kill anybody,' is going to convince a jury she's innocent. And you're a sturdy woman yourself, as my German parents would've put it. Fat-shaming is a dick move. I can't believe you did that in front of everybody."

Again, Trudi was direct, and sometimes direct was called for.

Ann's eyes widened in horror, and she put her fingers over her lips. From behind her hand, she said, "I'm so sorry, Bee. I didn't have time to think, and I just wanted people to stop saying that about you. It's absolutely ridiculous. We know that you didn't have anything to do with Ruddy's death, even though you were the person who found him."

Trudi stepped toward Ann. "I was there. You were there, too."

"Yes, but Bee was the one who suggested that we needed to go look for him," she said. Ann's lips pressed primly together.

"She needed a check to pay for the booze!" Trudi said, nearly snarling.

I lifted my hands to stop them from arguing. "Ladies' League is about to begin. We need to get onto the course to be in our places for the start time. Ann, I think you are starting on the fourth hole with Constance and Priscilla Sauveterre. Trudi, come on. We don't want to keep Moonie waiting on the seventh. She starts picking at scabs when we keep her waiting."

I herded Trudi in front of me, and we set off at a brisk pace to meet Moonie on the seventh hole tee box. When we got there, I had to use a bright pink golf ball because my bumblebee-colored soccer-style golf ball must have fallen out of my bag somewhere.

Somehow, I managed to hold onto my cool, and after the first few holes, Trudi and Moonie had me laughing and thinking about golf for the rest of the round.

CHAPTER 10

PAULINE'S COMMENT ABOUT how Ruddy had been delinquent on payments to other businesses rankled me.

Someone at his CPA business must have taken over and paid his bills there, but no one had taken over his bill-paying duties at Canterbury Golf Club.

I thought about it all day, all night, and into the next day, wondering how many businesses around town Canterbury Golf Club might owe money to.

There might be dozens of people who weren't being paid.

I might be bumping into people at the grocery store or my favorite Italian restaurant, and CGC might owe them money.

They might be blaming me from behind their smiles.

Or they might really need the money we owed them. Pauline had said that she had nearly lost her flower shop due to unpaid invoices, probably including ours.

I needed to find out who they were.

So I needed to see Ruddy's CGC accounts.

Besides, I had promised Constable Sherwood Kane that I would compile a list of people to whom the Canterbury Golf Club owed money.

Breaking into Ruddy's office was wrong.

I knew it was wrong.

And yet it was my civic duty to get that information for Constable Kane.

Breaking and entering was surely wrong.

But I didn't need to break anything.

Up on the clubhouse's second floor where my Lady Captain's office was, business offices lined the hallway, and we all just roamed around, sticking our heads in other people's offices, talking and drinking coffee while we caught up on all the little things that were necessary for someone to do if the club were to run smoothly. Most of the office doors on the second floor stood open during the day.

So, that Thursday afternoon when I was in my Lady Captain's office, I stood up and walked around.

Having Trudi with me would have helped calm my nerves, but she was sitting with her grandbaby that day. The little chub was all of nine months old and crawling like a puppy, and Trudi didn't want to miss a minute of it.

Sherlynne, the women's golf pro, was sitting at her desk in her office. I waved as I walked by, a casual wave that suggested I wasn't going anywhere important or doing anything interesting.

To act any more obviously nonchalant, I would have had to stroll with my hands folded behind my back, whistling something chipper.

Sherlynne waved back, but it seemed like she was concentrating deeply on whatever was written on the sheet of paper lying on her desk. She tapped the numbers into a calculator with a pencil.

I shouldn't disturb her.

Not that I was going anywhere important.

I was just going to see if Ruddy's old office was, maybe, unlocked.

There wasn't anything wrong with what I was doing. Walking through an unlocked door was neither illegal nor immoral.

Unlocked doors were essentially invitations.

I reached Ruddy's office and grasped the doorknob.

The doorknob did not turn under my hand, just stiffly clicked as I tried to twist it.

Of course, Ruddy's darn office was locked.

The one office that might help me was locked.

But it didn't have to stay locked.

I pulled my keys out of my pocket and sorted through the jangly bunch of them.

The rumor was that most of the offices on the second floor had been keyed to the same key because Ruddy had cut corners wherever possible to save money.

I inserted my key for my door to the Lady Captain's office into Ruddy's doorknob, and it turned easily.

Now, it was an open door, and walking through an open door was not illegal, as I had already established. Entering an office that was currently not assigned to anybody and taking a look around to perhaps solve a crime, provide closure to his family, and save the reputation of the club had to be a good thing.

And maybe people would stop whispering that I'd killed him, too. That would be nice.

Inside, Ruddy's office was bigger than mine, which was odd because as the Lady Captain, I spent more time at the club than Ruddy did. He was just a member of several committees and could write checks because he was a financial officer for some of those committees, but he didn't hold an official, albeit volunteer, position.

His window was bigger, too.

And his sheer curtains were newer.

Not that it was a competition or anything.

Still.

Plaques hung on Ruddy Agani's wall, listing his name and golfing accomplishments, such as winning low-net at the member-guest tournament three years ago and being on the team that placed second in the men's league a few years before that.

A laptop lay closed on Ruddy's desk.

Pale powder filmed the top of his computer and the desk,

sticking to smudges and whorls on the plastic and polished wood. Clear squares, where the dust had been removed, disturbed the even layer.

A forensic technician must have been in there to dust for fingerprints, probably Saturday morning when I'd seen Constable Sherwood Kane and my two ex-students on the seventeenth green.

I opened the laptop computer, wishing I was wearing my thick winter golf gloves to conceal my fingerprints.

Not that I had anything to hide.

I wasn't even sure what I was looking for.

Maybe I shouldn't have been in there.

I sat down in his chair and clicked on the spreadsheet software icon on the bottom menu of the screen so I could see which files had been recently opened. One was labeled *Canterbury Discretionary Money,* so I clicked that file to open it.

A solid wall of numbers filled the screen.

I blinked, backing up a little in the chair.

My college major had been elementary education, not math. The jumble of numbers and decimal points seemed like a whole lot of digits in one place. Just looking at all those numbers made my brain feel garbled.

So many, *many* numbers.

The only part that wasn't numbers was the left-most column, which was a list of business names, and the top row of headings.

My goal was to see whether I could tell if any other

Jessa Archer

vendors needed to be paid. If they did, I could find Erick
Walters or someone else and get them to write a bunch of
checks because surely this was an emergency.

Okay, accounting software. As a kindergarten teacher
for thirty years, I had mostly used a double-entry accounting
ledger to keep track of grades. Even in kindergarten, children
receive grades, and grades must be tracked. Otherwise, some
helicopter parent will demand to know why little Jimmy got
a star-minus in alphabet recognition instead of a star-plus.

It was only when I was ready to retire that those
newfangled, grade-tracking computer programs like
PowerSchool and GradeBook had become available. I had
used them a bit when the administration had forced me to
during my last few years of teaching, so I had a rudimentary
knowledge of spreadsheet programs.

Looking at this morass of numbers, I realized how very
rudimentary my spreadsheet knowledge was.

This looked like the Matrix.

I hovered over the tiny rectangles on the spreadsheet.
When I scanned my eyes over the screen, they just looked
like rows and rows of numbers. However, when I clicked on
a cell, long equations full of dollar signs, abbreviations,
arithmetic signs, and Greek letters were actually written in
there, and all that added together to make the numbers that
I saw in the boxes.

However, being a teacher in the olden days before
grade-tracking programs does lead one to acquire a certain

skill set.

One essential skill is adding long, long rows of numbers quickly and accurately. Everyone hates the end of the grading periods when every teacher stays up late to calculate those last few grades.

The longer you teach, the more efficient you get at adding long, long rows of grades.

I was quite good at it.

The problem was that when I scanned those long rows of numbers, the sums on the ends didn't add up.

Computers should be able to add numbers correctly, right? That was the whole flippin' point of these oversized calculators.

I clicked on the number at the end that should be the sum of the row, and the whole row before it highlighted. The equation buried under the number should make that number the sum of the row.

But it wasn't.

The actual number, which was supposed to be all the previous numbers added up, was too high every time. Some were inflated ten dollars or so, but one was several thousand dollars higher than it should have been.

That was weird.

When I tried to inspect the long equations, some of the references went to other pages of the spreadsheet.

When I clicked over to look at those pages, they were blank.

Why would Ruddy have blank pages in the club's accounting spreadsheets?

I deleted the page.

On the first page, the numbers in the last column changed to red hazard triangles.

That was bad.

I did the control-plus-Z thing that undoes whatever you did that messed everything up, even if you don't know what you did.

The numbers came back.

Which meant there were invisible numbers on that other spreadsheet, the blank one.

I went back to the spreadsheet that appeared to be blank and clicked on a cell. When I clicked an empty square, text appeared in the Name Box, the box at the top where you type in what you want into the computer, but the cell still *looked* empty.

Someone had hidden numbers in the spreadsheet by making the text color the same white as the white background. Not even highlighting the cells revealed the text written in them.

Well, that was easy enough to fix. I selected-all on the page and changed the font color to black.

The boxes still looked empty.

It hadn't worked.

When I looked up in the corner of the page, a little padlock denoted that the page was locked and thus was read-only.

Well, chicken gizzards and fries.

At least I could still see the contents if I clicked on them.

As I clicked around on different boxes and looked at the top of the screen, I found numbers, amounts, and names.

The names that I found in the first column going down were the club's vendors, like our florist and the carpet-cleaning people.

The numbers in the fourth column varied, but most were a few hundred dollars.

Oddly, most of the numerals were round numbers, like $50.00 or $200.00, rather than the precise numbers you would expect to find on a complicated invoice that included labor, materials, and taxes.

This looked like someone had been padding invoices, adding a bit of money to each one.

Had Ruddy been stealing the club's money?

And yet, even if it had been tens of thousands of dollars, no one at the club would have killed Ruddy for skimming money from the club. The Canterbury Police Chief was a club member, as was Constable Sherwood Kane. We would have had Ruddy arrested and sued him to get the money back. The club membership included several lawyers, too, like Oliver Shwetz.

Oh, no. Ruddy had been arguing with Oliver Shwetz at the glow-ball tournament before he had been killed.

It still didn't make sense. If Ruddy had been skimming

off the club, any club officer would have just called Constable Sherwood or the police to arrest Ruddy.

Plus, Oliver Shwetz was just a club member. He wasn't an officer or on any boards or committees, and he didn't have the power in the club to write or approve checks or do anything with money. Oliver was just one of the members who paid dues, played golf, and ate food in the clubhouse.

No, that altercation looked like it had been personal.

Well, now I had two possible motives for Ruddy's murder: a personal one because Ruddy had been so unpleasant to everyone he met, including Oliver, and a possible criminal connection because Ruddy might have been skimming money from the club.

I scowled at the computer. The darn thing had complicated my investigation instead of helping it.

Investigation.

I almost smiled to myself as I closed Ruddy's computer, hearing the crisp click as it closed.

An ex-kindergarten teacher and golf club Lady Captain couldn't investigate a murder. How amusing.

And yet, I was being forced to investigate Ruddy's murder because people thought I had killed him. My reputation and the reputation of Canterbury Golf Club were at stake.

So, I was cornered.

I scowled at Ruddy's computer, mad at Ruddy for getting himself killed.

A Murder at the Country Club

A man's voice said, "Good afternoon, Bee. Who unlocked Ruddy's door for you?"

CHAPTER 11

I GLANCED UP from Ruddy's computer, startled.

Erick Walters, the club's treasurer, was leaning against the doorway, his long legs crossed at his ankles. His relaxed smile seemed unassuming, like he didn't suspect me of trying to cover up a murder by messing around with Ruddy's computer, thank goodness.

I had so many guilty thoughts.

Erick said, "I've been trying to get in here for days to see what was going on with Ruddy's accounts. What'cha doing?"

"Oh, hi." I stood up, brushing off my golf slacks and giving myself a minute to think. "Just remembering a few years ago when Ruddy won"—I squinted and read the plaque again—"the low-net prize at the member-guest tournament. He was so proud of himself."

Erick laughed. "Yeah, he was proud that he had brought in a ringer to win it. I still think paying the pro from New

Scot Links golf course to play with him was right on the edge of cheating."

Oh, yes. That had been the year that Ruddy had brought in a ringer, because the next year, the membership had approved a rule to ban paying PGA professionals to play as "guests" for the member-guest tournament.

Erick had argued for the new rule, I remembered, standing up in front of the all-member meeting and announcing, "If you don't pass this rule, I will mortgage my dang house, and my *guest* for the member-guest tournament next year will be Tiger-*freaking*-Woods."

Some members did take club tournaments *very* seriously.

Erick asked, his tone light, "Did you find anything interesting on Ruddy's computer?"

"You're a CPA, right?" I asked.

He laughed. "Yeah, but I'm a lapsed CPA. I hated accounting. Long rows of numbers, stupid spreadsheets that made their own errors overnight, and the clients. Dear Lord, the clients. I do not miss a minute of it. Selling real estate is my calling."

I flipped up the lid on Ruddy's laptop. "Have you ever seen anything like this?"

Erick walked around the desk and squinted at the screen. He pulled his neck backward like a cat about to cautiously bat at a bug. "Forgot my readers."

"I can make the font bigger."

"No, don't change anything. I'm not even sure we

should be in here. I'm surprised that the police didn't take his laptop."

I wiped my finger through the gritty powder on the desk. "They dusted for fingerprints."

He nodded. "And this is a small town. I'm not sure what kind of resources the police department has."

"Constable Kane said that they sent the knife to the state forensic laboratory."

"Oh," Erick nodded. "The one with my fingerprints on it. Great."

"Your fingerprints? Oh, did you actually touch it before Trudi could warn you off?"

Erick's eyebrows crumpled in, and his mouth pressed in a rueful, embarrassed smile. "I thought I would pick it up to give to the police. Seeing Ruddy lying on the ground dead really freaked me out. I'd never seen a dead person before."

"Yeah, it's weird, especially your first time. I imagine even more so when it's a murder."

"Have you seen a deceased person before?" Erick asked, peering at the computer screen.

My hands wove themselves into a knot in my lap. "My husband had his stroke while we were eating lunch at home."

"Oh." Erick glanced up at me. "I'm sorry. I forgot."

"No, I'm okay." It wasn't okay. I wasn't okay. But my grief makes other people feel bad, so I don't talk about it. Instead, I said, "No one lives forever, and we had thirty good years. Some people don't get a quarter of that." I was getting better at saying it. "I wanted to show you what I found on this spreadsheet."

"You shouldn't be looking at this, anyway. You can tell who edited the document."

"I'm not editing anything," I said.

"Yeah, but see? You can tell." Erick clicked over to the Review tab and clicked something saying *Notes*. "Holy cow! Who are all those people?"

A long list populated down the page. Quite a few of the names were familiar. I mused aloud, "Nell Rinaldi, Sherlynne Orman, and Trudi? Everybody on there has been making changes on this spreadsheet? No wonder it's all messed up."

Erick squinted and leaned back. "These are all the people who have permissions to make changes." He pointed. "Oh, it's because they have check-approval power. Anybody who can approve checks can make changes to the top sheet, but the other sheets are locked. You can tell by the little padlock on the tab. Why aren't you on here?"

"Because I don't have check-approval power, I guess."

"Yeah, but you opened the spreadsheet. It should know that you're looking at it."

"It's Ruddy's computer. It can't tell who opened the spreadsheet, just who's logged onto the computer." I glanced at the webcam hole in the top of the screen, which might be spying on me. "Right?"

"Oh, yeah." Erick sounded relieved. "That must be it. I'm just always paranoid about accounting. The Gnostic Yacht Club that we belonged to got sloppy with their accounting, and someone embezzled a hundred thousand dollars from them a few years ago. That's why they closed."

"Is that why they shut down?" I asked him. "That's shocking."

"It was very hushed up," Erick agreed. "I was on the board. I managed to avoid doing any of the financial stuff there, which is hard to do for an accountant, even an ex-accountant. Everybody assumes that if you were a CPA, you must like looking at spreadsheets." He gestured at the laptop's screen. "This gives me hives."

"So, you didn't have anything to do with the money there?" I asked.

Erick shook his head. "Nope. I might have caught on if I'd had access to the records. I mean, *maybe*. I don't know how well they were hiding it."

"I didn't realize that you were a member there, too."

"We quit about a year before it fell apart. I admit, though, that I didn't like being part of a club where something like that went on, but the main reason we quit was that you can't have two side hustles. Golf is a harsh mistress, and between men's league, committees, club tournaments, and just playing, not to mention range time and lessons and committee commitments, I was spending a fortune and all my spare time over here. Our oldest, the sailor in our family, went away to college. Afia was getting tired of paying to maintain a boat that we only used when he came home, so we gave up sailing for golf. There are a lot of people here who were members over there, though. Sailing and golf are hobbies for people who have the money, and a lot of people do both."

"Like who?" I asked.

"Oh, the Sauveterres joined up here after the yacht club went under. LaMonde Jackson and his wife stayed at the yacht club right up until the bitter end, I heard. The Carmos, the Damirs, the Shins, and Berkowitzes. Lots of people."

"I never knew that. Now, with all your magical accounting skills, can you see which of the vendors we have paid and which ones we haven't?" I asked him. "Someone has to pay our bills. We have to task someone else with that job."

Erick frowned. "I'm paying the bills."

"For the electric and the water bills you said, right? But not for the ones that require approval like Jacob's package store."

"Oh, that's what you're looking at. Maybe if we sort the spreadsheet data by the date of approval or bill-paid—"

I lifted my hands off the keyboard and backed right up. "You do it. I'll mess it up."

Erick swiveled the laptop toward himself, though I could still see the screen. "If we do this," he did something, "then, there! All these bills without a date in this field"—he pointed at the screen—"have not been paid."

Hundreds of them.

My stomach turned acidic at the thought of all those people in town who needed their money. "Oh, no."

"We'll have to task someone to pay those bills, I guess."

"Are they all approved by a committee member?"

He squinted at the screen. "If this box is initialed, then yes. You can see who initialed it, and it should match their log-in credentials in the note."

"Good. Can we get someone to pay all these bills at the next board meeting?"

Erick bit his lower lip. "I suppose that's the best way to do it."

"Well, we need to. I'll just print out a copy of the—Dear sweet holy baby in a manger, how do you make this thing print?"

Erick laughed and clicked around. "What do you want printed?"

"Just the names, addresses, and amounts of people we owe money to." Erick clicked, and I heard a mechanical whine from down the hallway. "Constable Kane wants a list of them, too."

"There you go, then. They're all printed out. If you need anything else, let me know."

"Thank you, Erick. I appreciate it."

His wrist, right beside my hand, buzzed. "What was

that?"

He tapped the watch, and it stopped. "Oh, it's one of these new-fangled watches that connects to your phone. My son made me get it because he has one. That's my wife calling. I'll call her back. It tracks my steps and my sleep, too."

"Oh, cool. I don't have a new-fangled watch."

He smiled and cocked his head to the side. "My brother is divorced, you know. If you wanted to meet him for coffee, he would appreciate it. I would appreciate it."

Oh, all the saints. How would I get out of this one? I ventured, "Does he golf?"

"Sadly, no."

"It would be a waste of his time, then. Thanks, but no thanks. And thank you for your help with the computer, Erick."

CHAPTER 12

BACK IN MY Lady Captain's office, I swiped and tapped my phone screen until it rang up Trudi.

The printed-out spreadsheets littered my desk. On some of them, the ones with white-on-white numbers, thin lines cross-hatched the page, but they were otherwise blank.

My office walls were painted a nice, restful shade of dark green, as befitted a golf-based country club. Maybe I should hang some of the plaques that I'd won in there. They were sitting a box in the garage, gathering dust.

"Hello?" Trudi's voice squeaked out of my phone. A baby cooed and gargled in the background.

"Hey, do you have a minute?"

"Sure, let me put you on speaker. I have my hands full. Yes, I do. Yes, I do. Full of *grandbaby.*"

Trudi was completely smitten with her grandbaby Nigel, and her smittenness was just the cutest thing in the world. "I'm waiting."

The timbre of the sound coming out of my phone hollowed out, and Trudi's voice said, "Okay, go ahead."

"I found something weird when I was looking at the club's spreadsheets," I told her.

"Oh? Math?" Trudi relished being everyone's resident nerd whenever they needed math or science explained in small words.

"Yeah, there are a bunch of formulas that take data from other sheets in the file, and then those sheets have weird formatting so that you can't see what someone has written there."

"So, how do you know it exists?" Trudi asked.

"The numbers and words were formatted as white text on a white background, so you can't even highlight them. If you click on the cell, though, you can see what's written there in the little box at the top."

"Nice sleuthing. Good job, there."

Warm happiness wafted through me. It's not every day that a PhD-level ex-neuroscience professor compliments your ingenuity. "So, that's weird, right?"

"Very weird. When can I take a look at them?"

"I have print outs of the ones you can see. I have blank pages of the white-on-white ones."

"Print-outs? Not the computer files?"

"No. I was going to drop them into my cloud drive but didn't get a chance. Erick Walters barged in on me and took over."

"Yeah, he does that."

"Can I drop by sometime? Or could we meet at the club for lunch?"

She asked, "How about we take a look at them over lunch at the club tomorrow, and then we'll play nine?"

Trudi never let me down. "Sounds great."

CHAPTER 13

AFTER LUNCH, AS Trudi and I sat at a round table far in the back of the clubhouse, she snagged a piece of bacon off my plate that had fallen out of my sandwich and crunched down on it. Her eyes rolled up in her head as she sucked on the crisp meat. "Oh, my word. *Real salt.*"

I tugged the spreadsheets out of a shopping bag. "About these spreadsheets."

"Yeah," Trudi said, pushing her empty salad plate to the side. "Let's take a look, or maybe we should sneak into Ruddy's office again. I'm kind of sad that you did that without me."

"But your hands were full of grandbaby."

She grinned. "Yeah, they were. So, let's see the pages."

I fanned the paper across the table. "You can see here, where I had a cell selected, that the formula in the cell isn't a simple sum of the row."

Trudi flipped through the pages, scowled, flicked back

and forth between sheets of paper, circled some numbers in black, and finally sneered at it. "Jeez, that's inefficient. Look at that formula up here that was in the Name Box when you printed the sheet. It's pulling data from four other sheets in the document, and they're all the same type of data. All this could have been on one sheet and just summed with one pull of the cursor, but no. The references go here," she pointed one blunt, sensible fingernail at a square on one page, "here," pointing at another box on another page, "and way over here." She dragged her finger down a column of digits. "This is ridiculous. It's so ugly."

I nodded as if I had understood the spreadsheet well enough to have come up with that thought, myself. "Yes. Definitely."

Trudi threw an amused glance at me. "It's like it's *deliberately* complicated."

"*Oh.*"

"Yeah."

"That makes all kinds of sense."

"Sure does."

"But who would want to hide something from the club?"

Trudi raised one gray-blond eyebrow at me. "Someone who is stealing from the club."

"Was Ruddy stealing?" I asked. "Do you have evidence of that from these papers?"

"I can't be sure," Trudi said, "but either somebody was trying to hide something, or whoever managed these sheets was incompetent or dumb as a box of rocks."

"Ruddy was a certified public accountant," I reminded her.

"I don't see how that changes what I said."

"Oh, Trudi," I laughed. "Surely, Ruddy wasn't incompetent."

"That leaves—" she prompted.

"No, no. Surely he wasn't that, either."

"I'm not so sure." Trudi tapped the papers on the table. "He didn't pay people on time either, and that's one of the basic job skills for being a CPA."

"But that's because he was cheap."

"Or maybe he couldn't figure out whose bills were due because he was incompetent."

"Well," I said, wincing, "that would change things a bit."

"Or maybe because he was stealing from the club and trying to obfuscate."

That would be horrible. "And that would change things a lot."

"Yeah. What's this?"

"What's what?" I leaned over to look at where she was pointing.

Her finger rested on one of the blank spreadsheets, a waste of paper and printer ink that I'd almost dumped into the recycling bin rather than tote down to lunch. The tip of her fingernail pointed to the Name Box at the top, where the text that was in the selected square showed up.

The word in the box read, *Oliver Shwetz.*

"That's weird."

Trudi looked up at me, peering at my face. "When I was in the lab, when someone said, 'That's weird,' we'd all look up because it meant they'd found something unexpected, and perhaps, something important."

"Yeah, well, it's weird that Oliver Shwetz's name would be on these spreadsheets, right? He isn't a club officer, and I don't think we retain him for any club business, right?"

"Not that I know of."

And Trudi probably would know. She had a finger in pretty much every committee in the club.

"Huh," I said.

"Yeah, *huh.*"

I gathered the pieces of paper together. "I wonder if there's any way to find out."

"Oliver Shwetz must know why his name was on these spreadsheets," Trudi said.

"But it's not like we could just come right out and ask him."

"If we talked to him, maybe we could figure it out."

"I don't think that's a good idea," I told her. "He might get angry."

Trudi mused, "I think I saw his name on the afternoon tee times list for around two o'clock. I think we should play golf with him and casually work it into the conversation."

I shredded my paper napkin like a naughty

kindergartener caught cutting Play-Doh with scissors. "I don't think that's a good idea at all."

But Trudi was already striding toward the staircase to the second floor.

CHAPTER 14

AFTER A QUICK consultation where neither of us divulged any real information, Sherlynne Orman finagled the tee times list and added Trudi and me to Oliver Shwetz's twosome. We met them on the first hole's tee box to tee off.

I whispered to Trudi, "I don't like this."

"It's just golf." Trudi was dragging her little hand-cart that held her clubs behind her. She sometimes called it her *sportsing stroller* when she was pretending that she was a non-sports-oriented, intellectual nerd. She asked, "What could be wrong with playing golf at a golf club?"

"Still," I muttered, but I pushed my clubs and cart toward the first hole's tee box.

I was surprised to see that my uncle, Arnold Holmes, was Oliver's playing partner that Friday afternoon.

I probably shouldn't have been surprised. My uncle Arnie was a talkative extrovert and would play a round of golf with just about anybody, although he usually preferred to shepherd ladies around the course. He liked ladies, and they liked him. However, all his flirtations came to nothing, which had always seemed odd to me. "Uncle Arnie!"

"My favorite niece," he said and returned a quick cheek-kiss. "Are you walking out with us today?"

"Yep, playing nine holes. I need to smack a ball around with a steel rod to blow off some steam."

"Wonderful." He leered over my hat to see who was behind me. "And you brought company?"

Trudi frowned at him. "Put your eyes back in your head."

"As you wish, my lady."

Trudi rolled her eyes. Arnie was probably doing it to get a rise out of her. He was easily old enough to be Trudi's father and maybe her grandfather, and Trudi was married.

And all Uncle Arnie's flirtations came to nothing.

We shook hands with Oliver, who had looked fidgety ever since Sherlynne had strutted over and informed him that ladies would be joining them that afternoon.

The guys at the club grumbled a bit about Ladies' League taking up prime tee-time real estate on Wednesday mornings, but the guys didn't dare say anything about women playing golf. Indeed, most of them were more than welcoming during the rest of the week, at least to our faces. I'd always suspected that most of them had the ulterior motive of trying to get their wives to play. Though almost all of them would deny it over beer, when their wives came to play, they fell all over themselves to make sure their girls had a good time. Most of them wanted to golf with their wives because they missed them and because they had probably noticed that the guys with golfing wives played a *lot* more golf in total.

Normally, Oliver was fine with women golfing with him. Indeed, I'd golfed with him a dozen times or more.

But that afternoon, he looked twitchy.

I grinned at him. "Hey, Oliver. As one prime suspect to another, how're you holding up?"

He sighed, but he looked less worried once I phrased it like that. "Not too well. I hate everyone looking at me like I'm a murderer."

I nodded. "I hear you on that. I'm catching all kinds of flack. Nell practically accused me in front of the whole Ladies' League, though Ann and Trudi stood up for me." I glanced at Trudi, and she smiled back at me.

His shoulders deflated. "These people have known me for years. I went to elementary school in this town. I had Mrs. Toltinetti for kindergarten."

"I remember her." Mrs. Toltinetti had retired a year after I had begun teaching. She'd worked at the school for forty years.

"I've been everyone's attorney for decades. You know what they say: all attorneys are sons of guns, but your attorney is *your* son of a gun. I've advocated for half of Canterbury."

"And you've advocated *against* the other half of Canterbury," Trudi said, because she had no filter.

"Trudi! Don't worry about it, Oliver. When they catch the real killer—"

"Heavens to Betsy, that sounds guilty," Uncle Arnie said as he inspected the few clouds drifting across the sky.

I continued, "As I was saying, when they catch the real killer, then everyone will be sure it wasn't one of us, and they'll be sorry they suspected us. Has anyone said anything to you?"

Oliver kicked a wayward tee that was lying on the ground. "The other three guys of my usual foursome got here an hour early today and forgot to text me. They're already on the fifth hole."

"Oh." That was mean of them. "Well, instead, you get to play with us, and we're much better golfers than they are."

"Yeah." He still looked dejected.

"Come on. Let's tee off."

One by one, we all hit our first balls into the air. The white dots soared down the fairway.

Uncle Arnie traipsed off into the thick grass to find his, while the other three of us walked down the middle of the smooth fairway to where our balls were staggered.

Trudi set up to hit hers again first, holding the smaller club in her tiny hand as she bent over and peered down the fairway. "So, Oliver, why was the club secretly giving you money?"

A Murder at the Country Club

"What?" he shouted and stepped backward.

"Jeez, Trudi," I said. "Oliver, she didn't mean anything by it."

Trudi swung her club, and her little ball bounced down the grass in the middle of the fairway. "Hey, I'm not accusing him of murder, but his name was hidden in some very convoluted spreadsheets. Who was secretly giving you club money, and why?"

"The club never has paid me any money," Oliver said. "I've never filled out a timesheet to invoice the club, and I haven't done any work for the club itself. I've never received any money from the club in any capacity."

"You know that right off the top of your head, huh?" Trudi asked him.

"Maybe now isn't the time," I told her.

From somewhere over in the rough, a swishing sound whispered over the course. The whiff was followed by a muffled curse that was not a whisper and was definitely the expletive of an older man who had fought in wars. *"—that devil ball!"*

Oliver scowled at Trudi. "I keep mental notes in my head and comprehensive lists back at the office of places that I have not worked for, and therefore it would not be a conflict of interest for me to sue them," Oliver said.

I felt my head tilt with disbelief. Defending a lawsuit right now would destroy CGC. "Were you planning to sue the club?"

Oliver shook his head. "Oh, no. I'm not *planning* to. But you know, you have to keep a mental list of places that you don't have a conflict of interest with. I am *scrupulous* about legal ethics, and legal ethics are primarily about whom you have taken money from. I try so hard to stay clean with attorney-client privilege and billable hours and conflicts of interest. I also don't have a conflict with the grocery store, bowling alley, or the ice skating rink. Especially the ice skating rink. That's also why I haven't served on any club committees. It would be a conflict of interest if I were a club officer and then sued the club."

From over in the rough, another swish and a string of truly imaginative profanity echoed over the bright fairway of the first hole.

Trudi asked Oliver, "Then why would your name be hidden on a spreadsheet that Ruddy had made?"

I touched her arm and whispered, "I don't think we should do this."

Oliver's eyes narrowed. "I have no idea. I would tell you to ask Ruddy, but someone killed him for all the shady stuff he was up to."

"How do you know that he was into shady stuff?" I watched Oliver carefully.

His dark eyes bugged out a little, and he flung his arms around with emotion. "Because he's dead. People don't get dead unless they're into shady stuff."

"Oh. So, you don't know it for a fact," I said, relieved.

"Well, I assume he must have been. Everyone knows that he was delinquent paying bills, and—"

Trudi asked him, "What did Ruddy Agani say to you at the glow-ball tournament?"

"Privileged," Oliver spat out.

"Why was he so mad?" she pressed.

"Privileged," he growled, getting even more angry.

"Why do you think Ruddy was dirty?" Trudi asked.

I listened while Oliver recounted Ruddy's past crimes—all of which were actually occasions of being impolite and not paying vendors on time—and took my stance over my ball, readying myself to hit it down the fairway. It was all stuff that Trudi and I and everyone already knew, from Ruddy delaying payments to small business owners to him shorting people just enough that it wasn't worth going to small claims court about.

More old-man swishing and cursing sailed through the warm, clear air.

A golf club bounced across the fairway behind us, turning end over end and flashing silver in the sunlight.

I smacked my ball hard, and it rolled up onto the edge of the green, leaving myself a long putt for a birdie.

We walked up to even with Oliver's ball and waited for him to take his stance over on the right side of the fairway.

Oliver waggled his golf club as he readied himself. "I don't know why you would even suspect me of that. I've been scrupulous about keeping away from any conflicts of interest."

Just as Oliver drew back to hit his ball, Trudi asked him, "So why was your name on Ruddy Agani's spreadsheet of embezzlement?"

Oliver swung and missed his ball, spinning around as he over-rotated. "Holy cow! I was in my backswing!"

Trudi continued, "From the position of your name on the table, you were listed as a vendor, and there should have been a list of paid amounts after your name. How much has the club paid you?"

"Nothing," Oliver spat as he picked up his ball and slammed his club back into his bag. "Nothing at all. Not a doggone cent. I've paid my dues to the club in full every quarter, and I don't appreciate being accused of having a conflict of interest. I should stop talking to people at this club. People ask me about this and that, who paid who and what amounts. I'm sick of you and Ruddy and all the other club officers threatening me just because I'm doing my job." He turned his pushcart of clubs around, back toward the tee box. "I'm not golfing today. Good-bye."

We watched him stomp back toward the first tee.

Shivers ran down my arms, and I toweled off the club heads sticking out of my bag to cover the shaking in my hands. "Oh, Trudi."

She shrugged. "I didn't think we would get anything out of him. No one's going to confess just because you tell them about one piece of evidence. He sure doth protest a lot about his ethics, though, and he protested about his ethics more than about being accused of murdering Ruddy."

"We accused him of embezzling from the club. By extension, we accused him of having a motive to kill Ruddy Agani. We also suggested that he isn't nearly as ethical as he insists that he is. I'm not surprised that he got mad."

Trudi regarded the long green fairway stretching in front of us. "Yeah, well, he didn't particularly do anything to make me think he *didn't* do it. He would have denied it either way. If he'd had business with the club, coming clean and giving us a reasonable explanation would have lowered our suspicions. But from what he said, he didn't give us any explanation about why his name was on a spreadsheet that was probably full of payments for embezzlement, which means he might be guilty."

I didn't like it, but I had to agree.

My uncle's robotic golf pushcart zipped up and stopped beside us, with my Uncle Arnie following it and thumbing his remote control. "Got out of the rough in one."

"That's amazing," I said to him. "Indeed, it's simply unbelievable."

He flicked his hand toward where Oliver Shwetz was stomping down the golf course. "Where's Ollie going?"

"He decided not to play today."

"Oh, needed more time to get ready for that inquiry from the state law board next week, did he?"

I turned and regarded my uncle. Sunlight showered over

his chalky skin polka-dotted with dark liver spots as he squinted toward the clubhouse. "I beg your pardon?"

"The state law board is investigating him for some ethics breaches. He has to appear before them next week. I forget which day."

"How do you know that?"

"Oh, you know. You talk with people while you golf. Sometimes, they say stuff they probably shouldn't."

"Who said that?"

"I couldn't say."

Dang it. Arnie was a cheating, gossipy old coot, but he held some of his best gossip close to his vest so he could pop it out for best comedic effect.

CHAPTER 15

AFTER TRUDI, UNCLE Arnie, and I finished playing our nine holes of golf without talking any more about Oliver, I grabbed my extra bag of clothes from the trunk of my car and took a quick shower in the ladies' locker room, scrubbing myself all over with the club's balsam shower gel to rub Oliver's anger off of my skin.

I didn't like it when people were angry with me, especially since Oliver was the one with a conflict-of-interest problem.

More club business waited for me in my office, so I trudged up there to work on more paperwork.

Part of my paperwork was a budget for the summer months, which was an exercise in optimism considering that the club was still running a major deficit. We needed more members soon, and I began listing the phone numbers of guests who had been at the First Annual Nighttime Glow-Ball Golf Tournament to call and ask if they had any questions about the club.

I should write a canned response for when anybody asked about the murder that night.

Perhaps something along the lines of reassuring them that the Canterbury police department was investigating and no one from the club had been indicted or arrested for Ruddy's murder.

Maybe that was too cold-hearted.

It felt cold-hearted.

And yet we needed to call these people if the club was going to survive.

My to-call list had grown to forty names when my cell phone rang. I didn't even look at the contact name displayed on the screen before I answered, which was always a mistake. "Hello?"

"Hello! I was wondering if you had a moment to talk."

I recognize the woman's voice right away, and I wished that I had never answered my phone. "Oh. Hi, Lale. It's so great to hear from you again. That was a really long piece you published in the *Canterbury Tales* about the club."

"That's exactly what I'm calling you about. I'm calling all four of you who found Ruddy's body that night."

A groan nearly escaped my throat, but I coughed instead.

Lale said, "I was hoping that you had more information on Ruddy Agani's murder. Do they know who did it yet? Do you hear any gossip in the club that might be important?"

A Murder at the Country Club

"The Canterbury Golf club has no information, and we do not have a comment at this time. Please contact the Canterbury Police for more information about this matter or any other crime." I thought that sounded rather professional and hoped it would end Lale's questions.

"I've already talked to them. They won't tell me a thing. However, I'm writing another article about the murder—"

A huge sigh floated out of my lungs, but I managed to cover the phone before Lale heard me.

"—Because it's the most interesting thing that's happened in Canterbury in years."

Yes, it certainly was, and it was the very worst time of all for the Canterbury Golf Club to be featured as an interesting story.

"I can't use family gossip, of course, so I have to look for other sources."

Family gossip? "Are you related to Ruddy Agani?"

"Oh, yeah. He was my uncle. As a matter of fact, since he cut two of his kids out of his will six months ago, I'm going to inherit quite a bit of money from him."

I rocked back in my chair and grabbed the edge of my desk to keep from falling over backward, my feet pointing at the ceiling. Lale Kollen, who had been at the glow-ball tournament, would inherit money if Ruddy Agani was dead?

I wanted to press her.

I wanted to ask her every question that was boiling in my head.

I wanted to stand up in a crowded room and point to her and insist that she confess.

However, Lale Kollen could write another scathing article about Canterbury Golf Club, which would ensure that no one in the small town of Canterbury would be interested in joining the club.

So, I said, "I am so sorry for your loss."

"Well, it's not much of a loss. He was awful at family get-togethers. He could start a fight with anybody. I'm not surprised at all that he started a fight with Oliver Shwetz that night. At Thanksgiving last year, he started a fight with both of his grown kids who had left town, three of my cousins, and my aunt Virginia Cohen. His kids haven't come back since, not even for Christmas or Easter. I thought Aunt Virginia was going to deck him."

"You don't mean Virginia Cohen who lives over on Pink Myrtle Street? She knits afghans for orphans and single-handedly buys most of the food for the food bank over in New Thames."

"He accused her of doing all that just so other people would talk about her. She also helps refugees from war zones get settled, you know?"

"I didn't know that," I said.

"Aunt Virginia tries to keep stuff quiet. Anyway, I would have thought that half of my family had a reason to murder Uncle Ruddy, except that most of my family lives out of town now because he drove them out of Canterbury."

I couldn't help myself, but I instantly regretted asking, "So, you are one of the few members of his family who was in Canterbury that night, right?"

Lale's voice dropped an octave as she asked, "Are you implying something?"

"Oh, no. Of course not. I would never suggest such a thing, and it seems like there are too many suspects as it is."

The long pause on the line suggested that I had said too much.

Lale asked, with an artificial lightness and a smile in her voice, "Other than you and Oliver Shwetz, who else is a suspect in the murder of Ruddy Agani?"

"I didn't mean anything by that. It's just a figure of speech. The Canterbury Golf Club has no comment at this time about the untimely and tragic death of Ruddy Agani. I'm so sorry for your loss." I jabbed at the red dot on my phone to hang up the call.

My cell phone's screen went black, and I sucked in air, panting at how stupid I had been.

When my racing heart slowed, I called Trudi so I could make her tell me that I hadn't been stupid and hadn't ruined everything.

After she answered the phone and I finished confessing what I'd said, Trudi sighed and said, "Well, she's going to run with that piece of information. I can hardly wait to see what she writes in the *Canterbury Tales* tomorrow morning."

"I can't believe I said that. I ruined everything."

"I think it's interesting that she gave herself a motive for killing her uncle. She could've easily grabbed a knife from any one of the dinner tables right in the clubhouse and gone outside after Ruddy. She'd even seen Ruddy and Oliver have an argument, which would throw suspicion off of her. This is weird."

"There are just so many people who wanted to kill him," I said. "I hope I never make that many people angry at me."

"Oliver Shwetz had that argument with him right there in public. Pauline Damir hadn't been paid for months and was about to lose her business. Ruddy's wife, Linda, was ready to divorce him and leave," Trudi said.

Footsteps plodded down the hallway toward my office. "It's like you're keeping a list."

"It's the ex-scientist thing, again. I tend to keep a running list of alternate hypotheses. Did I forget anyone?"

I shrugged, even though Trudi couldn't see me over the phone. "Anybody else he owed money to. Evidently, quite a few of his family members, including his adult children, disliked him. Even Virginia Cohen had words with him."

"Virginia Cohen, who lives over on Pink Myrtle Road and spends most of her pension buying supplies for the food bank?" Trudi asked.

I nodded. "Yep, *that* Virginia Cohen."

"Wow, you've got to be some kind of a jerk to make *Virginia Cohen* mad at you," Trudi muttered.

The footsteps were right outside my door now. "Hey,

Trudi, I've got somebody coming toward my office. I can hear the intent to talk to me in their footsteps. Toodles."

We hung up.

Sherwood Kane stepped around the edge of the doorway and into view. He leaned against the side of the door frame, his strong arms crossed over his burly chest.

I force a smile onto my face. "Hello, Constable. What can I do for you today?"

CHAPTER 16

SHERWOOD KANE GRINNED and walked into my office. He never wore a uniform, of course, because he wasn't a police officer, just an elected official who oversaw the town's interests in a lot of different matters. "Have you killed anybody else lately?"

I rolled my eyes. "Sherwood, I told you that I didn't kill Ruddy."

"Oh, I'm just kidding around. I can't imagine you killing anybody." He poked one finger around the arm of the small chair that I kept pushed against my office wall in case someone dropped by to talk. "I just stopped by after playing a round of golf to see if you found that list of people that the club owes money to because Ruddy wasn't paying them."

"Oh, yes. I managed to dig that up." I dug the printed spreadsheets out of my desk. "Here you go."

Sherwood folded the papers and tucked them in one of his back pockets. "Not that we're making much headway in the case anyway. The state forensic department still hasn't analyzed the murder weapon for fingerprints."

"Just so you know, they're probably going to find Erick Walters' fingerprints on that knife. When we found Ruddy, he bent over and grabbed the knife to pick it up before we could tell him not to touch it."

Sherwood Kane tugged his phone from his hip pocket, touched the back to open it, and started thumbing the screen. "Okay, I'll tell them you said that, but that doesn't mean we can rule him out as a suspect. He might have touched that knife when you could see him specifically to explain his fingerprints on the knife from when he killed Ruddy."

"Oh, dear. I hadn't even considered that Erick Walters might be a suspect. That brings the number of actual suspects up to five," I said.

Sherwood squinted at me. *"Five?"* Other than you and Oliver Shwetz, who are the other three?"

"I didn't do it. I told you that I didn't do it, and so there are four more suspects, other than Oliver."

"You've been busy, haven't you?"

"It's important to know who killed Ruddy because his family needs closure." That was a really good reason. It sounded much less guilty than saying that I needed to find the real killer, and it sounded a lot better than the fact that I was just worried about my golf club.

Sherwood held his phone, ready to take notes. "Okay,

tell me who you think did it."

"Okay, so Oliver Shwetz had that argument with him, but he went up in my office after their argument. He didn't follow Ruddy out to the course."

Sherwood tapped notes into his phone. "You said that he was up there alone, and when you went up there, he was missing. That was during the time when Ruddy might have been killed."

"I feel bad about gossiping about Oliver because I heard that the state law board was investigating him for violations of their code of conduct. He got really mad when someone accused him of a conflict of interest. It seems to be a sore spot with him. Does anyone know what Ruddy and Oliver were arguing about that night at the club?"

He shrugged. "I've talked to a few people who were standing around, but no one overheard what they were talking about until Ruddy got mad and started yelling, and then everyone heard that. Who else do you think are suspects?"

"Pauline Damir and anyone else whom Ruddy's CPA business or the club owed money to. She said in front of everyone in Ladies' League that if someone else hadn't taken over Ruddy's accounts after he died and paid her, her florist shop would've gone out of business."

Sherwood frowned and took some more notes. "That's thin, and as you said, he owed a lot of people money."

"And Ruddy's wife was going to leave him. Linda had

already rented an apartment in California to move out there."

"How do you know that?"

"She came in to make sure that their club membership had been canceled."

"How very pragmatic of her. Was she at the glow-ball tournament?"

"No. She and Ruddy had a fight, and she drove around in her car afterward. I don't know of anyone who saw her here."

"Great, 'driving around' means no alibi," Sherwood grumbled as he thumbed that information into his phone. "Doesn't anybody just get divorced anymore? And who else?"

"Lale Kollen, the reporter from the *Canterbury Tales*, who was at the club that night. I certainly wasn't hanging on her to make sure that she didn't leave at any time. I know that she saw the argument between Oliver and Ruddy, and she had a chance along with everybody else to grab one of the club's steak knives."

He didn't look up while he entered the information. "Why would Kollen kill Ruddy Agani?"

"She just told me on the phone that she is Ruddy's niece and stands to inherit a substantial sum of money from him because he disinherited two of his adult kids."

"Sounds like the kids have more of a motive because he cut them out of the will."

"Revenge, yes. Money, no. They were already out. Besides, they all live far away. They haven't been back here since last Thanksgiving."

Sherwood typed it into his phone, but he looked up at me, frowning. "I don't want to say this, but you sure are going to a lot of trouble to find a whole crowd of different people who might have had a reason to kill Ruddy Agani."

"Because his family needs closure."

"Two of his family members are on your list of suspects. That doesn't sound like you want closure. That sounds like you are trying to throw suspicion on other people."

"Sherwood! I told you that I didn't do it, and I can't believe that you would think that I am capable of such a thing."

"One of the things that I do not like about this job is that I get more suspicious every year. I read a lot of the police reports, and it seems like the nicest people commit the most horrible crimes. You are right, Bee. You are one of the nicest people. A few years ago, I would never have believed that somebody like you could do anything like this, but this job gets to you. It really gets to you."

"Well, maybe you need somebody level-headed with you when you go ask these suspects about Ruddy's murder. I could go with you when you question them, and I could give you a second opinion."

Sherwood winced and shook his head. "Bee, you and Oliver are still the prime suspects until we have evidence that says otherwise. I'm sorry, but I can't let one of the major suspects go with me when I ask other people about their whereabouts and motives."

That made sense, but it still made me mad. "I still can't believe that you would think that I did such a thing. I was a kindergarten teacher." Meaning that surely I was the most harmless person in town.

He chuckled and tucked his phone back in his pocket. "Yeah, if a roomful of five-year-olds won't make you snap, nothing will."

"Oh, Sherwood. That's not what I meant."

He stood and stretched, bending his elbows because his hands would have pressed against the ceiling in my office. "I know, and I don't like suspecting you. I can't let one of the prime suspects go with me, though. I am sorry, Bee, but you should stop investigating this because it makes you look worse."

CHAPTER 17

TWO DAYS LATER, on Sunday, my uncle Arnie texted me and suggested a round of golf that afternoon, which meant that he had some important gossip he needed to tell me right away, not that he would ever admit he was the club's biggest gossip.

The first few holes that we played were uneventful, our balls flying through the air and landing on the soft grass that smelled like summer in the bright sunlight. We made some putts, we missed others, and we talked about nothing of particular importance until I started grumbling that only four people had signed up for the club's monthly Nine and Dine scheduled for the next Friday night, and that included Trudi and me.

That seemed to be his cue that he had waited long enough to divulge the gossip that was burning in his soul.

Uncle Arnie scratched his cheek where his white beard was growing in. "Well, you kinda can't blame them. The number of people playing rounds of golf here has dropped dramatically, too."

"It has? I hadn't noticed. Everybody was at Ladies' League on Wednesday."

"Were they, though?" he asked, tilting his head as we walked toward where our balls had landed.

"Most of them were. A lot of them, anyway." I thought harder about the small group that had gathered on the practice green to hear my pre-round announcements. "About half of them, I think."

Maybe half.

"That's better than the men's league. Only three foursomes went out, and we usually have fifteen or more."

That was so bad. "I haven't heard of any more membership resignations, other than Linda Agani, of course."

"Oh, they haven't quit, yet. I think they're waiting and watching to see what happens with the police."

"They're going to be waiting for a while. Constable Kane said that the Canterbury police haven't even gotten the forensic report back from the state laboratory yet. I haven't even heard that they've been questioning anybody."

"No, but that reporter has been calling people up and asking questions."

"And I don't know what good it would do if the police did question suspects. Even that reporter," I gestured at my uncle, agreeing with how he had brought Lale Kollen into the conversation, "had a motive to kill Ruddy. She's his niece, and she's going to inherit some money from him. And she isn't a club member. Nobody was ever murdered here before, but the one night that Lale Kollen is around, suddenly somebody dies. I think that's suspicious."

"And I've been asking around," Uncle Arnie said.

I touched his arm as we walked down the fairway. "Really? Have you heard something?"

"Nothing of importance. Nothing that would help out, particularly. I just heard that people are nervous. Having a murder at the club has set everyone's nerves on edge."

"But they aren't planning to resign their memberships, right?" I asked.

"Nope, not yet. But I'm worried that if the police don't turn up something soon, people might not be interested in hanging around as members. That Greens of Grass Country Club down the way is set to offer yet another membership special, I've heard."

"Oh, no. We can't lose any more members. If we lose anybody else, we are going to have to cut the budgets for all the committees, including social and maintenance. People won't like that. If we don't have social events and other country club benefits, people will start quitting the club."

Uncle Arnie laid his arm around my shoulders and jostled me around like he had when I had been a teenager and too obsessed with the high school quarterback. "I'll talk to 'em. I'll let them know that the club is safe and you are working on making sure that Canterbury Golf Club is still the best place to belong. And don't you worry about Ruddy Agani's murder. I am sure something will turn up soon, and everything will get back to normal."

His confidence should have been infectious, but I was more worried about the club than ever.

CHAPTER 18

AFTER GOLF WITH my uncle, I grabbed my satchel with extra clothes from my car trunk, showered in the ladies' locker room, and ran into the operating budget committee meeting in the dining room at the last minute, trailing the green scent of the balsam soap and shower gel that the club supplied. I needed to get home soonish because the foster kittens had begun eating some solid food, and they needed to be fed. "Hello! Sorry, I'm late!"

The other eight members of the operating budget committee were seated around two of the long tables that had been pushed together to make enough seats for all of us.

Erick Walters smiled at me, though he was tapping his pencil point on the papers scattered in front of him like he had a case of nerves.

Trudi grinned and patted the chair beside her, so I bustled around the table to sit between her and Erick.

The other people—Nell Rinaldi, Matthew Johnson,

Mina Shankar, and more—had various reactions, from Nell's studious glare at her phone to Mina reaching behind Erick and patting my shoulder with a smile.

"Quick meeting," Trudi said, standing up. She was only slightly taller than when she had been sitting down. "We have a few things to approve for the operating budget. Shoreline Landscaping says that we need four more yards of mulch for the parking lot planters and that new flowers will be needed every month instead of every six weeks due to the increasing heat. Erick pushed back, but they are adamant. It's either cough up the money or take bids and do the vetting and voting all over again." Groans emanated from everyone at the table, including me, at the thought of the hiring process for a new landscaper. "All in favor?"

I joined everyone else in saying, "Aye," even though we all eye-rolled while we did it.

Three other items had to be voted on, so we did.

The board discussed a new contracting process, as it seemed like too many people from various committees were overlapping in duties. The clubhouse committee wanted to pick a new carpet-cleaning vendor because the current one was insisting on bi-monthly deep cleanings, which both cost too much in this time of financial troubles and closed the clubhouse to members too often. However, picking a new vendor required a liaison from the operating budget committee, and all of us shrank in our seats and didn't look up when Trudi asked for a volunteer to liaise.

Finally, Trudi said, "Come on, guys, Ann Carmo is the liaison from the clubhouse committee, and she needs someone *today* to approve her pick for a new vendor. It's just a cursory look and a sign-off, not a long-term obligation."

Since it was Ann, I started to raise my hand, but Lois Ngani beat me to it. I dropped my arm, relieved.

At the end of the meeting, Trudi said, "That's the end of the agenda. New business?"

I put forward, "I would like to nominate DeShawn Johnson, the club manager, to go through the list of outstanding bills and cut checks for every account that is currently in arrears."

Trudi said, "All in favor?"

Everyone at the table said, "Aye," except DeShawn, who said, "Hey! Wait a minute!"

"All opposed? Okay, the motion is carried."

"Wait a minute!" DeShawn said.

"I have a list of accounts and how much," I told him. "It shouldn't take more than hour, tops."

He frowned but didn't say more.

I swept my papers into a pile and pushed my chair back to stand.

Erick Walters said, "One more thing." His new-fangled phone-watch buzzed, and he frowned and tapped it, turning it off.

I lowered my butt back into my chair, wondering how my kittens were doing.

"There are some problems with the computer accounting spreadsheets," he said.

Sighs and groans filled the air.

Nell said, "I don't know how computers work."

Matthew added, "Can't we get a professional to do that?"

Lois said, "Call a computer repair person. None of us can fix computer problems."

"That's not it," Erick said, frowning. "It seems that some members of other committees have been logging onto the master approval spreadsheets and adding extra pages."

He must mean those pages that we had found on Ruddy's computer that looked blank but weren't. I settled back down and prepared to back him up.

"Aren't the masters set as read-only for most of the pages?" Trudi asked. "When I log in, most of it is read-only, except for the pages for the few committees where I have invoice-approval authority."

"Yes, but this is something else," Erick said. "I think someone else is gaining access."

"If someone's getting into them," Trudi said, standing up, "have Sherlynne change the passwords and hand out new ones. I have to get home. I'm babysitting this evening. Have a good weekend, everyone."

Erick caught me on the way out as other members were filing past us, while Matthew and Nell rearranged the tables back where they should be. "It's those pages we found."

"Yeah, I figured that," I said.

"I got back into Ruddy's office and computer, and I sat there and clicked on each box and wrote down what is in each one. There are just lots and lots of names, both people's names and business's names. I tried changing the background to black so that the white font would show up."

"That's smart," I told him.

He grimaced. "It didn't work. The font, color, and background on the sheet are locked."

"Oh, dang it."

Erick shoved some papers into my hands. "I found handwritten spreadsheets in Ruddy's desk with the same information on it as I was writing down. He was going through and clicking the boxes individually and writing down the contents, too."

The papers in my hands slipped, and I grabbed them before they fell. It was, indeed, pages and pages of spreadsheet print-outs. The tiny boxes held names of people and businesses, but no numbers. "This is weird. I've never heard of Canvas, Inc. or Rope International. We don't even use rope, right? And our deck outside is concrete. We wouldn't need anything from Deck Varnish, LLC. What the heck is Wilber and Friends or Shipmo Corp? This is a small town, and I've never heard of them."

"There are no numbers, no costs, no invoice or check numbers, just a bunch of names in weird white-on-white. I don't even know which committee's purview all this would fall under."

"Okay," I said. "We should tell Trudi about this. She's on most of the boards and committees. She'll know whose jurisdiction it is."

But Trudi was already out the door, off to see her grandbaby.

Erick said, "I'll look into it further. I don't know what to make of it, though."

I nodded. "Surely, we can figure it out, even though it might be nothing."

He took the printouts back from me. "Okay. I'll just put these back in my office for safekeeping."

CHAPTER 19

THE NEXT DAY was a mishmash of things I had to do and thoughts I didn't want to think about my friends at the Canterbury Golf Club. Even the thought that one of them might be a murderer was driving me insane.

Who would I even suspect?

Perhaps my uncle Arnie, the octogenarian club gossip and lady-golfer chaperone?

Maybe I should suspect my best friend, Trudi, who was on all the club committees and practically kept the club running from an organizational standpoint.

Maybe the murderer was Sherlynne Orman, the lady pro, who ran the pro shop with an iron hand and whose accounts balanced perfectly to the cent every month. That was as suspicious as a perfectly organized sock drawer.

Or maybe Pricilla Sauveterre had killed Ruddy. She was a newish member, and yet I couldn't see her taking the risk of getting blood splattered on her very chic golfing attire.

Jessa Archer

But perhaps it had been my frail and pale friend Moonie, who had used to be the school librarian where I had taught kindergarten. A librarian might know exactly where to stab someone with a steak knife to kill them. Reading all those books might have armed her with dangerous knowledge. Granted, she transported spiders outside rather than kill them and quoted Gandhi to unruly middle-schoolers, but if we were suspecting everyone, it might be her.

I sighed.

No, our real suspects were the guy that Ruddy argued with, Ruddy's wife, and the florist who was thrilled to get her money: Oliver, Linda, Pauline, and Lale Kollen.

Not that any of those people seemed likely, either.

Why did it have to be a club member at all? Perhaps a wandering vagabond had killed Ruddy. They still had those, right? Or maybe he had been murdered by a serial killer, one of those pasty-white guys who haunted late-night television and true-crime books.

Suspecting all of those people at the club was ridiculous. I couldn't bear to have those awful thoughts in my head, so I simply refused to think about them while I ate my breakfast and dodged my negative-nelly neighbor, Coretta Dickinson, who was skulking around the sidewalk in front of the house, watching to see if I was home.

So, I didn't open the front-window curtains and drank my coffee in the dark and in peace.

My mama cat needed feeding, and I picked up and

snuggled each one of her tiny kittens in turn, socializing them. Doing things like this was the important part of my life. I needed to concentrate on socializing the kittens, running the Canterbury Golf Club Ladies' League, and doing the other few things that I did to make myself a useful citizen in society.

Indeed, at that very minute, one of the club's more elderly members, Mrs. Eleanora Jones, called me on the phone and asked if I might have a chance to swing by and drive her over to the club for lunch and golf in the afternoon. A number of our members were no longer able to drive, due to eyesight or other health considerations, but that didn't mean they couldn't play golf. All of them still wanted to play, even those who called the game Devil Ball. Therefore, we other club members who still had our driving privileges tried our best to chauffeur these elder statesmen to the club whenever we could. I ended up driving people to and from the club at least once a day. I didn't mind.

Indeed, I told Eleanora that I would be over in about an hour to pick her up.

Eleanora's call was practically a sign from the heavens, a signal that I should mind my own business and keep to my schedule, rather than poke my nose into police investigations where I wasn't welcome.

After dressing in golf attire, I made sure I had my keys and other necessary things as I went outside to get into my car and drive Eleanora to the club.

See? I wasn't thinking about anything other than my own business at all. I had put those other things completely out of my mind.

As I stepped out of my front door and turned to make sure it was locked, my foot slipped slightly.

I looked down at my welcome doormat.

A newspaper was lying on my front step, and my foot had slid on the paper when I had stepped on it.

The newspaper was, of course, the *Canterbury Tales, Monday Edition,* and the headline read, "Canterbury Golf and Murder Club."

Drat, that Lale Kollen had written another story about Ruddy's murder.

Everyone in town was going to read it.

Our club members would stay away even more.

No new members would sign up.

My teeth ground against each other.

Obligations came first, so I drove over to Eleanora's house to pick her up and drive her to the club. We chatted amicably during the short drive, although I think I was less successful at hiding my anger at Lale Kollen than I would have liked.

Eleanora kept asking me if the kittens were all right and if there was anything she could do to help me with club matters.

When she asked for the third time if something was bothering me, I reached into the back seat of my car, snagged that horrible newspaper, and dumped it in her lap. "I can't believe that Lale Kollen wrote yet another article in the *Canterbury Tales* about what happened to Ruddy Agani. I mean, it's terrible. Of course, it's terrible. We invited Lale Kollen into the club as a favor to *her*. She's the one who needed more local stories. She contacted *us*, not the other way around. Now, not only did she write one sensational article about this horrible tragedy, but now she's written another one just a few days later."

Eleanora peered at the newspaper and frowned. "This does seem to be taking matters too far. 'Golf and Murder Club,' indeed."

"This is *insane*. Lale Kollen is *insane*," I said, watching the road but shaking my head. "She keeps calling people who were there and coming up with these stories. She called me a few days ago and wanted to know if I'd heard anything around the club about who might have killed Ruddy."

"Well, she is a journalist. I imagine that's what they taught her in college," Eleanora said.

"But she was there when Ruddy was killed. She saw Oliver and Ruddy arguing, and people weren't keeping an eye on her. She might have gone out after him. Maybe she did it."

"I would hate to think that about that young lady," Eleanora said.

"She could have grabbed one of the club's steak knives. It didn't have to be a club member."

"I suppose that is so."

"And now she's latched onto writing about Ruddy's murder like a hungry pit bull, and she won't let it go. Everything in that newspaper is going to be about the club and how Ruddy was murdered at the club. Maybe she's trying to throw suspicion onto someone else. When you think about it, being a reporter is a great way to deflect suspicion by accusing other people. Did you read the article?"

"I'm looking it over right now," Eleanora said. "It doesn't seem to say anything new. It seems like all the facts are the same as they were a few days ago, that Ruddy was killed with a knife and no one knows who did it."

"She shouldn't keep publishing about the club. This is *harassment.*"

"Oh, nothing ever happens in Canterbury. I suppose we shouldn't be surprised that there is more than one newspaper article about the only scandalous thing that's happened here in the last ten years. Why, when those high school kids toilet-papered the principal's house, there were three articles about that, not to mention the letters to the editor demanding that they be put in juvenile detention."

"This is harassment," I repeated, grinding my teeth together. "I should go down there and have a word with her."

Eleanora turned in her seat and squinted at me just as we turned into the golf club's parking lot. "I don't know if that's wise, Bee. You don't want to stir up a hornets' nest and make them think that there's more of a story here than there is."

I helped Eleanora get her little satchel out of the back of my car. Her golf clubs were stored in the bag room at the club, so we didn't have to wrestle them in and out of my trunk. "I'm going to go downtown to that newspaper and give them a piece of my mind. At the very least, they should stop harassing the club. Maybe Lale will say something incriminating if she did it."

Eleanora frowned, her dark skin already beading with sweat in the summer swelter. "Bee, perhaps we should just let this article go. If there's a third article, then maybe someone should have a word with her editor or something. In any case, if you suspect she's violent, I don't think you should confront her at all."

I opened my car door and tossed my purse back inside. "I'll be back to pick you up in four hours or so. This shouldn't take long."

CHAPTER 20

THE BUILDING THAT housed the *Canterbury Tales* was an old, red-brick structure on the banks of the river. The original building had probably been constructed in the late 1800s, but renovations, additions, and reconstruction had produced a much bigger building that housed several of Canterbury's businesses.

Inside, the stale air seemed to hover, even though ribbons on the air conditioning vents fluttered. Some of the walls had been stripped, and the exposed, antiquated red brick was crumbling in some places, whereas others were plastered over with modern drywall.

I passed the orthodontist's office, where teens slouched in the waiting room, and a small café serving soy lattes and vegan pastries before I found the wide, marble staircase for the upper floors.

The *Canterbury Tales* newspaper occupied the entire second floor of the building. A receptionist's desk was stationed in front of a long wall of frosted glass, behind which shadowy figures floated and merged. A single, closed door in the same material interrupted the diaphanous glass.

A black-haired man sat ramrod-straight at the reception desk, his hands spread on the frosted glass. The burgundy polish on his nails was expertly applied and unchipped. He drawled, "Can I help you?"

"I hope so," I said, trying to be brisk and pleasant. It wasn't this guy's fault that a reporter had written a hatchet piece about the Canterbury Golf Club. "I'd like to see Lale Kollen, please."

He picked up a tablet and looked at it. Sharp lines cut into his hairstyle like the prim set of his mouth. "Do you have an appointment?"

"No, but I was hoping Lale would see me. I already know her. I'm the one who helped her get into Canterbury Golf Club for her big exposé. She called me Friday. I have some more information to tell her."

The man gently set his tablet on his frosted glass desk, the bottom of it squared to the edge nearest to his pressed dress shirt. "I'm sorry. I can't allow you back into the newsroom without an appointment."

"Could you please call her and tell her that Beatrice Yates is here and has more information that she was looking for?" I hoped that would do the trick.

He glanced down at his tablet and sighed. "I suppose."

The man made a big show of dialing a cell phone and

beeping through extensions. He looked straight into my eyes, unblinking, while he listened to the phone for several seconds before tapping the screen. "She's not picking up."

I pulled my cell phone out of my purse and found Lale's contact information. A few taps later, I listened to her phone ring and ring until I gave up, too. I asked the man, "Has she been in today?"

"I wouldn't know."

"Wouldn't she have to walk right past this desk? Wouldn't you have seen her if she came in?"

"Maybe."

"Is there someone you can call to see if maybe she's in the ladies' room and will be back in just a minute?"

"No."

I gritted my teeth and opened up the web browser on my phone. Within a minute, I had found the *Canterbury Tales* website and the editor's phone number. I tapped my screen and called her. "Hello, this is Beatrice Yates. I am one of Lale Kollen's sources for her ongoing Canterbury Golf Club story. I have some important information for her." The important information was that she should stop writing the stories about CGC, and I was planning to record the conversation on my cell phone in case she did say something that would incriminate herself. "It's vital that I talk to her right away. Your gentleman here at the reception desk is not allowing me to come inside. Can I come back there and talk to her?"

Jessa Archer

"Lale Kollen hasn't come in today," the editor, Wendy Mack, replied in her gruff voice. "She uploaded her story from home yesterday afternoon on account of the weekend, but she probably had to go to the gym or get her nails done again or something."

"Can I leave a message with you or with your gentleman here at the front desk?" I smiled at the man. He did not smile back.

"Not sure what good that will do if she doesn't come in. Maybe a better option would be for *you* to tell her that *we* are looking for her."

A beep over my phone meant the call had ended.

I smiled at the man at the front desk, trying to charm him even though I knew it wasn't going to work. "She said that I could leave a message with you, and that you would put the note on her desk for me."

The receptionist lifted one eyebrow. "Fine. I'll take a message and put it on her desk when I have a minute."

Even though I knew the message was going to end up in the wastepaper basket beside his foot, I dutifully wrote a perky little note, telling Lale that I had some important information for her and asking her to call me at my cell phone number, which I also wrote down.

When I left, I knew that effort had been a spectacular waste of time. Maybe hunting down Lale Kollen at her house would produce better results.

Oh, I probably shouldn't say it like that, *hunting down Lale,* because everyone thought I killed Ruddy.

I'd only said it in my head, right?

But I had no idea where she lived.

Canterbury wasn't a teeny-tiny town where everybody knew everybody, but it was a small town where surely somebody would know someone who knew that person.

It wouldn't take me long to find out where she lived.

As I exited the building into the warm morning air, I tapped my phone and dialed a number. "Hello? Uncle Arnie?"

CHAPTER 21

BY THE TIME I got to my car, three text messages from three different people had popped up on my phone, all of them with the same address, the one for Lale Kollen's house.

Uncle Arnie hadn't known where she lived, but as I'd suspected, he knew people who knew.

Driving over to Lale's neighborhood took only a few minutes through some middle-class areas of Canterbury. Small houses with nicely tended yards lined each of the residential streets, and I drove slowly because children wearing bathing suits were running through sprinklers in the warm summer afternoon.

As I parked on the street in front of Lale's house, I reminded myself that my primary purpose was to convince her not to write any more stories about the Canterbury Golf Club.

But just in case she said something to incriminate herself because she was the real murderer, I would record everything that we said with my cell phone. Confessions were no use unless they were recorded in the murderer's voice. Just me telling the police wouldn't be enough. I'd watched enough movies to know that was true.

A car stood in the driveway, a coppery sedan with local license plates. I didn't know what Lale's car looked like, but the hood seemed sun-warmed under my palm as I walked past, but not hot as if it had recently been driven.

As I walked up her short sidewalk to the front door, I turned on the voice memo recorder on my phone. I whispered into it, "I, Beatrice Yates, will now go knock on the door of Lale Kollen's house, and I am recording this in case it becomes evidence in a court of law."

That sounded stupid, but at least I had something to establish what was going on.

Even though it was noon, Lale's front porch light was lit, a bright spark of light in the shadow from the overhang of the house.

I also told my phone the date and time, in case that was important, even though the app probably had some sort of a timestamp.

"I will now knock on Lale Kollen's door and ring her doorbell." No reason to stop saying stupid things now.

As I rapped on her white-painted door, the wood moved under my knuckles.

The door swung open, and my last knock missed the wood entirely.

That was weird. I hoped that everybody had given me the right address.

"Lale? Are you here?" I called.

There was an odd odor in the house, maybe like a cat box needed cleaning.

"Lale!" I held my phone up near my face as I stepped inside her living room to make sure that my voice was being recorded. The front room was decorated in clean lines, mid-century modern. The dark blue couch stood on silver feet that matched the silver rod-and-glass coffee table. A television hung on the pale green wall, surrounded by framed prints of ferns, fruit, and fairies. "Hey! I just wanted to talk to you about that article in the *Canterbury Tales* newspaper this morning. I'm not mad or anything. Are you here?"

A cat peeked around the corner of a wall and retreated. Quick scratching on the floor sounded like it had run away.

I closed the door behind me so her cat wouldn't get out.

"Lale! Are you here? Hey! Your front door was open. If you are not here, I'm just going to back out and leave. I'll catch you some other time." I realized I was talking to an empty house, but I took a few more steps inside. "Is anybody here?"

I leaned forward to peer around the edge of the wall and into the next room, the kitchen.

Bright stainless-steel appliances reflected the sunlight, but a dark stain and a woman's body lay on the white-tiled floor.

CHAPTER 22

"BUT I DIDN'T—" I gasped, holding onto the armrest as I sat in the passenger seat of Sherwood's car, sucking the air inside a paper bag. The paper rattled as I tried to get my breath.

Sherwood sat in the driver's seat but was twisted in his seat to watch me. "Breathe, Beatrice. Just breathe."

"I swear to God, Sherwood—"

"It's okay, now. Don't say anything else." His worried eyes watched me over the inflating and collapsing white paper that I held. The bag smelled faintly of french fries, but the man had produced a paper bag when I'd been hyperventilating. Paper-bag beggars can't be choosers. "Come on, Beatrice. Take your hands off your face. I know this is hard, but please calm down so that you don't make anything worse."

"But you heard the recording. I had just gotten there. I walked in. There, she was. It was horrible!"

"The recording does back up what you told us. Personally, I don't think that scream on your recording could have been faked, but it's not like it's physical evidence. Some people might think you staged it."

"*But I didn't.* I didn't even know where Lale lived until I asked my uncle Arnie where her house was. And then people sent me texts. There are timestamps on those texts. Didn't that police officer say that she had been killed hours ago? Something about the blood or her body was cold or something? Oh, my Lord. *Oh, my Lord.* I can't believe someone killed Lale Kollen."

"I know it's odd—"

"Things like this don't happen in *Canterbury.* No one kills journalists *here.* That sort of thing happens in Russia, or third-world countries, but not in *Canterbury.* "

He said, "Beatrice, you know that I like you. I have to advise you to stop talking. You found *both* of the murder victims. That looks bad. It looks like you knew where the bodies were because you killed them."

"I *didn't.* I would *never*—"

"Of course not."

"I have to call someone to pick up Eleanora at the club and take her home. I have to feed my cats. I have to socialize the kittens."

"Don't panic. Breathe into the bag."

"You think I killed her, and I'm going to go to jail, and I have to drive Eleanora home!"

"I don't really think that, but some people are paid to be suspicious. Several people knew that you were looking for the second victim. You've already told us all the people who will corroborate that you were looking for the second victim."

"I was looking for her because I didn't know she was dead!"

"Beatrice, please. Don't say any more."

"I didn't touch Lale after I got there. My fingerprints probably aren't even on the doorknob because I knocked and the door opened in front of me. I didn't touch anything else in the house. My fingerprints shouldn't be on the murder weapon. So, shouldn't that prove that I didn't do it?"

Sherwood nodded. "If we find someone else's fingerprints on the knife, then it would certainly support that someone else killed her."

"But it's going to take *months* to get the fingerprints back on this knife, too, isn't it? Why do murder investigations take so long? No one else here has anything to do. There hasn't even been a shoplifting incident this summer for them to investigate."

Sherwood fidgeted in his seat, sighing. "We received the forensic report on the knife that killed Ruddy Agani."

I dropped my hands away from my face and stared at him, livid. The paper bag crumpled in my lap. "Why didn't you tell me that?"

"The police department does not advertise developments in an ongoing investigation. Besides, I'm not a police officer.

I'm just the Town Constable. It's not my job to decide when and whether to release that information."

"What is your job, really?"

He sat back in his seat, and his eyes were a little more amused. "As far as I can tell, it's to get reelected. Other than that, I attend the Town Council meetings and speak for law enforcement."

"So, speak for law enforcement now."

"It's not like that."

"Whose fingerprints were on that knife?"

"I'm not sure we should be talking about this."

"My fingerprints should not have been on that knife. I did not touch the knife that night, and I think there's a low probability that someone snatched my knife from dinner. Besides, I don't think I even touched my knife at dinner. I had the lobster."

Sherwood nodded. "Fine, fine. I can confirm that your fingerprints were not found on the knife." His firm voice sounded like he had carefully constructed that sentence.

"How would you even know what my fingerprints look like?" I asked him. My friend Trudi knew what my fingerprints looked like, but she didn't forget anything, ever.

Sherwood shrugged, and his shoulders lowered in relief at my line of questioning. "You were a kindergarten teacher. All school employees have to be fingerprinted for background checks. When that state law about child molesters went into effect a decade or so ago, you and everybody else at the elementary school gave us their fingerprints. Lots of other people's prints are on file, too, anybody working with kids in the school system or daycare, or if you apply for a liquor license or a gun permit, or if you are going through the citizenship process."

"Oh, yeah. I remember that. I was glad they didn't use ink to take them, but they just used that machine with a glass screen on it and the greasy stuff. Then, how can I be a primary suspect if you know my fingerprints weren't on the knife?"

"Because you could have wiped off the knife after killing Ruddy, just like you might have wiped off the knife here, too. We can't rule someone out just because we didn't find a piece of evidence. It might be there, and we didn't find it."

A horrible thought occurred to me. "Were *no* fingerprints found on the knife? Is that why you think I wiped them off? I didn't, though. I didn't touch either one of the knives or wipe them off. Erick Walters' fingerprints should have been on it, though. I saw him touch it that night, out on the seventeenth green. If they didn't find Erick's fingerprints on that knife, then they messed up the analysis."

Sherwood's lips tightened. "At least two sets of fingerprints were found on the knife," he ground out.

"But do you know whom they belong to? Everybody has fingerprints. Unless you were able to compare them to somebody's fingerprints, then you wouldn't know whose they were, anyway."

His lips thinned further. "One set of fingerprints found on the knife was identified."

I told him, "We know that one of them should belong to Erick Walters, but that doesn't mean anything because I saw him touch it after Ruddy was already dead."

Sherwood frowned for a second and then rubbed his cheek with his hand. "I should not be telling you this."

"But you're going to anyway."

"Erick Walters' fingerprints were found on the knife. He has a handgun permit, so we had his prints."

"But you know how his prints got on there, so you know he didn't do it."

"We know nothing of the sort. Walters might have picked it up so that his prints would be explainable when they were found on the knife."

"Well, I don't believe that. He was fine in the clubhouse before we found Ruddy. Whose fingerprints were the other ones?"

Sherwood stared out the front windshield of his car, his fingers clenching on his knees.

"Come on, Sherwood. You have to tell me."

Sherwood squeezed his eyes shut and bit his lower lip.

He looked like an overgrown kindergartner who was trying to hide a secret.

I opened my eyes wide, making sure that I did not look like I was squinty and out of control. The wide-eyes technique always worked on elementary school students.

"Sherwood, I need you to tell me whose fingerprints were on the knife, right now."

He sighed. "The other set of fingerprints on the knife was not identified."

His defeated body language—lowered shoulders and downcast eyes—suggested that he had told me the truth.

I asked him, "Seriously? You could've told me that. That's *nothing.*"

"The police might not want that information known publicly. They might want to try to use it to get someone to confess. So, you can't tell anyone that. That's got to stay a secret. It rules out a lot of people."

It certainly did. It ruled out everyone I'd worked with in the school district, like Moonie, my school librarian, and a lot of other people, too. "Pffft, Sherwood. Why would I bother to tell anyone that?"

I needed to talk to Trudi, and I needed to do it right then.

"Beatrice, I mean it. That's sensitive information."

I folded the paper bag and laid it on the dash of Sherwood's car. "I'll be prudent. When can I get my phone back?"

"They'll need to wipe it down for blood spatters—" he said.

"Blood spatters!" I wasn't sure I wanted it back anymore.

"—and they'll need to retrieve your recording off of it. In a big city, it would have to stay at the police station as evidence, but this is Canterbury. I don't think anybody really suspects that the town's retired kindergarten teacher killed two people. I'll see if I can get your phone back for you."

I wasn't sure whether to be insulted or relieved that the town police probably didn't think that I could have killed anybody, but I was really glad to hear that I would be getting my phone back.

CHAPTER 23

BACK IN MY little office at the Canterbury Golf Club, I wrote down everything that I could remember about what Sherwood Kane had told me.

Two sets of fingerprints were on the knife that had killed Ruddy.

One of them belonged to Erick Walters.

The other one hadn't matched any of the fingerprints that the Canterbury Police Department had on file.

That eliminated a lot of people.

I dialed Trudi's number on my cell phone and listened to it beep.

When she picked up, I started, "You will never believe what I found out today."

Trudi's voice was high and sing-song as she said, "Hello, my friend Beatrice! This is my friend, Beatrice! Beatrice has called me on the phone when I am babysitting my *grandbaby!*"

A high voice cooed in the background.

I tried very hard not to be jealous of Trudi's grandbaby. How can one miss what one never had? "Hey, it seems like I've caught you at a bad time."

"No time is a bad time if I have my *grandbaby!*"

"What time do you think you'll be done babysitting?"

"It looks like I will have my *grandbaby* until nine o'clock tonight and all day tomorrow. We could make plans to go to lunch after Ladies' League Wednesday?"

"That sounds great, Trudi. I'll text you later, and I'll see you Wednesday morning for league."

"I can't make Ladies' League this week. I have my *grandbaby* that morning, too. But I can probably be at the club in time for lunch."

"Okay, great," I managed to say. "See you then."

We hung up the phone, and I sighed. I wanted to get busy on figuring out who may or may not still be a suspect, especially when everybody was going to be eyeing me at Ladies' League on Wednesday, anyway.

On my office wall, my few plaques now hung. One of them announced that I had won low-net score for the Ladies Invitational Handicap a few years ago. One of them was for being a part of the winning threesome in a charity scramble over in Rhode Island.

Threesome.

Wednesday morning in Ladies' League, we would be playing *threesomes.*

Well, if I wanted to figure out whose fingerprints might be on that knife, maybe I should play golf with some of the suspects.

Sherlynne Orman was probably putting together the groupings for the league's shotgun start. If I caught her, I could golf on Wednesday with Pauline Damir, who had been on our list of suspects since the very beginning.

Pauline had never worked for the school district because she had started her own floral business when she had first moved to town. Certainly, a florist shop didn't need a liquor license, so it seemed unlikely that her fingerprints would be on file with the Canterbury Police Department at all.

Thus, it was possible that her fingerprints could be on the knife but that the Canterbury police hadn't been able to match them because they didn't have them on file.

Yes, Pauline Damir would be a great place to start.

I leaped up and trotted down the hall to the office of our golf pro.

Inside, Sherlynne was indeed slaving away over a spreadsheet with a pencil, figuring out who would play with whom Wednesday morning. "What can I do for ya, Bee? You don't have an opinion about the Ladies' League pairings, too, do you?"

"Actually, I'd love it if you could put me in the same group as Pauline Damir." I hoped that didn't sound too suspicious.

Sherlynne glared up at me. "Everybody has opinions

about who they will play with and who they won't play with. Every Tuesday, I get fifty phone calls dissecting my choices. Really, this should be determined by handicaps, rather than personalities."

"Fifty phone calls? Only about forty women played in Ladies' League last week."

"Yeah, some called more than once. Some of them call more than twice."

Setting the Ladies' League threesomes was similar to seating hostile guests at a wedding reception, except that it had to be negotiated every week. "If you could just pair me up with Pauline Damir, I would appreciate it."

"But if I take Pauline Damir away from her threesome, then I can't put Nell in there, because I was going to have Pauline play with Ann Carmo. Nell called me specifically and said that she didn't want to see Ann Carmo in her threesome. After that little scuffle before league last week, I don't think I'm ever going to be able to put them together again."

After what Nell had announced to the whole Ladies' League last week, I wasn't too enthused about the prospect of playing golf with her either. "Put Ann Carmo in with Pauline and me. Then you can put Nell in somewhere else."

Sherlynne sighed. "Fine. I'll just break up all these threesomes so you can play with Pauline Damir and Ann Carmo. Shotgun start at nine, as usual."

I swore to myself that I would get Pauline to either

confess or figure out why she definitely couldn't have murdered Ruddy Agani.

CHAPTER 24

ON WEDNESDAY, I steeled myself, gathering every bit of courage I could before Ladies' League.

The bag guys had already set up my clubs on my pushcart outside the door to the pro shop, so we were all ready to go. I grabbed my clubs and walked out to the practice putting green, which was warm with summer sunshine and dappled tree shadows.

But before we could begin, I had to make the usual announcements, so I grabbed the microphone and plugged it into the PA system. "Good morning, ladies! Here we are at the appointed place and time for our weekly round of golf together. As usual, there will be a nine o'clock shotgun start, but we are playing the back nine today. You should have all been issued your official score sheets. Note that today's game will be 'Secret Partner,' where one additional player's score will be added to your threesome's total to make a final score. All prizes this week will be awarded to the foursome, not individual players. Thank you for playing, and let's be careful out there."

High-pitched rumbling floated from the crowd of women as I stepped off to the side toward my handcart. I pretended to arrange the clubs in my bag even though they were all exactly where I wanted them to be rather than listen to what they were saying. I could vaguely hear Nell's voice, which sounded like she was saying something about me again.

I did not listen.

I really did not.

I not-listened so hard that I shut my eyes and rattled my golf bag, drowning out the hum of discussion.

Much closer, a woman's voice said, "Hi, Bee! I see we're playing together today."

When I looked up, Pauline Damir was standing right in front of me. Fuzzy pink head covers cuddled all her clubs like she had hand-knitted them, kind of like golf cozies.

I smiled. "Yeah, hi, Pauline. I hadn't gotten a chance to tell you that I appreciated what you said last week."

She flapped her hand at me, a shushing gesture. "Don't think another thing about it. It was ridiculous, what Nell was saying. But I think we shouldn't pretend that Ruddy was a saint, either, when he obviously wasn't."

There were so many reasons why Pauline might be disparaging the murder victim, including that he had dragged his feet in paying her money. "How's the florist business going?"

Pauline laughed. "It's going great! Ever since I have been getting paid for the jobs that I've been doing, I've been able to build my business quite a bit in only a few weeks. As a matter of fact, I'm doing a large wedding over in New Leeds this weekend. It's my biggest job yet."

So, Pauline's business had benefited from Ruddy's death and subsequent payment of debts owed, though several other businesses in town probably had, too. Pauline's florist business probably wasn't unique or even uncommon in that regard.

Behind Pauline, Ann Carmo trotted briskly over, pushing her own set of clubs. Her scarlet lipstick was especially glossy today, her bright red shoes were practically glittering in the sunlight, and her sunglasses were huge and dark. "Hello, girls! I see we're golfing together today."

"Hello, Ann. How are Wilber and the kids?" I asked her.

"About as well as can be expected. The older one is talking about marrying his girlfriend, though I assure you that I am not old enough to be a grandmother yet. So, we don't know what to think about that. The younger one is thinking about working on a tuna boat this summer, even though we pay her tuition and dorm. Wilber is Wilber."

I shook my head. "How did they grow up so fast? It seems like just yesterday you were quitting your job as my kindergarten aide because you were pregnant and wanted to stay home with your child."

"The real question is, how did we get to be so old? It does seem like just yesterday that I was working in the school with you. And then it seems like just this morning, I was making their school lunches. And suddenly, here I am, chasing this devil ball around the golf course to get out of the house because my husband has retired from his job and lost his other hobby, and now he's underfoot all the darned day."

We laughed. I tossed my new favorite golf ball—a white ball with pink hearts printed on it that Trudi had found in a water hazard while fishing for her ball and had given to me —in the air as we waited to walk out to our assigned starting holes.

As we were laughing and fiddling with our clubs, Erick Walters walked by, dragging his golf clubs behind him in a handcart.

He smacked his forehead with his palm. "Dang it, I forgot that Wednesday is Ladies' League day. You guys will be out there hitting the devil balls for what, two hours or so?"

I stepped toward him. "Two and a bit, usually. I'm sorry, Erick. It's on the scheduling whiteboard by the pro shop."

"I checked that yesterday, and all I remember is that Thursday afternoon is the high school team practice. It's probably on there. I just forgot about it. That's okay. I'll just drink myself into a stupor in the bar while I wait for you ladies to clear the course." His abused tone was so over-exaggerated that it was obviously meant to be a joke.

A Murder at the Country Club

We laughed at him, but Ann, Pauline, and I were all eyeballing each other and shrugging. With no head shakes in evidence, I said, "Hey, Erick, why don't you play with us? We can't use your score as part of Ladies' League, but at least you'll be able to play now instead of waiting for two or three hours."

Besides, then I could interrogate both Erick and Pauline at the same time.

And Erick played quickly. He wouldn't hold us up.

I was ashamed that it was a factor, but in Ladies' League, we get around the course in less than two hours for the nine-holers. We keep up the pace of play.

He asked, "Are you ladies sure? I wouldn't want to intrude."

"I think it's all right with us. Pauline? Ann?"

They both agreed that Erick could join us for our nine holes that morning.

He said, "I appreciate it. I've got a showing this afternoon that must not be rescheduled. That's probably why I forgot that you had reserved the course. I'm excited about tagging along and seeing the seedy underbelly of Ladies' League for myself. There are rumors, you know." He winked, and we laughed.

We headed out onto the course, as we had been assigned to start at the seventeenth hole. The morning sun blazed from above the trees, casting long, black shadows over the course as we walked out.

Just me, two innocent people, and a murderer. *Maybe.*

CHAPTER 25

THE GOLF COURSE was bright and sunny that day as we walked out to the seventeenth hole, which was our appointed tee box for the Ladies' League shotgun start. A shotgun start means that everybody begins their round of golf playing on a different hole, and then you play around the course until you get back to that hole. This format is more time-efficient than everybody gathering around on the first tee and having to wait while groups tee off in seven-minute intervals.

As I gazed over the green expanse and reed-choked water hazard on the right, memories of the night of the glow-ball tournament filled my head. We were right back on the seventeenth tee box that morning, looking down the fairway that led to the seventeenth green where we had found the body of Ruddy Agani.

I had played the Canterbury Club's golf course since Ruddy had passed away.

This wasn't the first time I had set foot on the

seventeenth hole.

Playing this particular hole with Pauline Damir gave me the creepy-crawlies up my spine, though.

And yet, what better place to get her to confess?

Having Erick and Ann with us seemed especially poignant, since they had been with me when we found Ruddy's body. Maybe, with the three of us reminiscing around the flagstick at the end of the hole, Pauline would be pressured into saying something.

It sounded like a good plan.

Yet, my back felt like someone had poured ice water down my shirt.

All four of us stood on the first tee box, staring down the fairway toward the green.

The seventeenth is a long par-four from any of the tee boxes. Hardly anyone reached the green in two. It usually took me three or so hits to finally dump my ball near the hole. Even the club's best golfers considered it a bogey hole.

Erick asked us ladies, "Who has the honor?"

He was asking who should hit their ball first. I said, "Since you're playing from the men's tees, you should go ahead. After you're done, we'll walk up to the red tees."

Erick pushed his tee into the ground and grabbed his back as he stood up, groaning.

Oh, I hadn't known that Erick had a bad back.

An odd thought insinuated itself into my mind: Had Erick hurt his back when he struggled with Lale Kollen when he had killed her, just a few days before?

No, surely not Erick.

Erick Walters was a nice guy. Surely, he wasn't a murderer.

I watched him.

Erick stood over his ball, waggling his long golf club, his driver.

He looked down the fairway and squinted in the sunlight and then back at his ball.

He waggled his club some more, loosening the tension in his hands and wrists.

He looked back down the fairway and then back at his ball near his feet again.

Waggle, look.

Waggle.

Loooook.

What on Earth had happened to Erick, who used to be a quick player?

The fingers of my right hand hurt, and I realized that I was gripping my golf ball so tightly I had left a thousand pockmarks in the skin of my palm and fingers from the tiny dimples in the golf ball.

Meanwhile, Erick was still waggling his golf club and staring at the fairway like it might have moved since the last time he looked up.

Suddenly, I couldn't picture this hesitant golfer acting on the impulse to stab anyone.

Waggle, look.

The insane image of Erick standing in the dark with a knife, waggling the blade and looking from it to Ruddy Agani's chest, back and forth, *waggle, look, waggle, look,* assailed me.

I coughed, trying to cover up the very dark humor that had tried to come out as a laugh.

And yet, what if Erick's recent case of nerves was remorse?

I always say that you don't really know someone until you've played golf with them, and a major change in their game can mean that they've had a major change in their lives.

Erick continued to waggle.

Beside me, Ann Carmo rubbed the side of her face and fidgeted from one foot to the other, looking at the sky. She caught my eye, and her head inclined toward Erick, as if asking, *What the heck?*

Pauline didn't seem to notice that Erick was taking forever to hit his first shot. Indeed, she smiled at Erick serenely.

Something in the back of my brain screamed, *Hit the flippin' ball, Sergio!* but I didn't say anything.

Maybe the seventeenth hole was making him nervous because he had committed a crime here.

Maybe two murders weighed on his soul.

Maybe he had grabbed the knife lying on the green that

night when we'd found Ruddy's body to cover up the fact that his fingerprints had already been on it, and the other prints that the state forensic lab had found were merely from some innocent person who had set the tables before supper.

These suspicions were driving me crazy. Everyone seemed to be a suspect, which meant I was surrounded by possible murderers. If I were in a movie, the murderer's theme music would have been playing all the time, every minute, like they were always just about to jump out and grab me.

I stared at the toes of my golf shoes, bright white leather against the emerald green grass, until I finally heard the *whack* that meant Erick had hit his tee shot.

Finally.

"Okay!" Ann said as the three of us ladies began walking toward the red tees, pushing our golf handcarts over the crunching gravel of the cart path. We really needed to pave the whole cart path because some sections were still lined with gravel, but we wouldn't have the money for that until our membership numbers returned to normal. "Nice shot, Erick."

"Oh, yes, excellent!" Pauline added. "That was an amazing shot, Erick."

Well, I wouldn't call it an excellent or amazing shot. It was a moderate drive that had landed on the right side of the fairway, but he had indeed kept it in the short grass. It wasn't a bad shot. "Yep, good job."

We ladies teed off at the red tees, as was customary, with no club-waggling.

While Ann stood on the elevated tee box, placing her ball and tee and getting ready to tee off, Erick dipped his head near mine and whispered, "I've been looking at those spreadsheets some more."

"Oh?" I warily watched Ann go through her pre-shot routine, picking a target and aligning the toes of her scarlet golf shoes with it.

Erick was right beside my shoulder. I couldn't even get a golf club out of my bag in time if he grabbed me.

Erick said, "There's another sheet that you need to see. Or somebody needs to, anyway."

I turned to him. "Like what?"

"Checks that don't match vendors."

Whack.

Ann had hit her ball, launching it down the fairway.

I glanced over to see her white ball rolling down the middle of the short grass. "Nice shot!" And to Erick, "Which vendors?"

Erick glanced over my head. "A couple of them. I'll talk to you later."

With a few more hits of our balls and a whole lot of club-waggling from Erick, we were all chipping onto the green of the seventeenth hole.

I tried not to remember the lump of Ruddy's body lying on the ground, nor the dark stain that had marred the grass in the light from our cell phones.

All of us were probably feeling the same way. Ann and Erick had been right there with me. They were probably seeing Ruddy's corpse in their minds, too.

As we stood on the flat-mown grass, I noticed that Erick and I had managed to overshoot the hole, and our golf balls lay far away from where Ruddy's body had been.

Ann and Pauline had chipped their last shots to right where Ruddy's dead body had lain.

That didn't mean anything.

The most likely explanation was that none of us were particularly good at our short games and needed more practice time at the chipping area.

Erick and I skirted the edge of the green to get to our golf balls. After some minor maneuvering to see who was farther away, I putted my ball from the fringe to quite near the hole, whereas Erick chipped up and left himself a long putt for his par. He took his stance over that and knocked it skittering across the shaved grass.

This hole was almost over.

No one had confessed yet.

I should say something around Erick and Pauline to make one of them confess.

If only I could figure out what that was.

I opened my mouth and sputtered, "So, wow, this is weird, huh?"

I was not good at this interrogating stuff. Kindergartners

were so much easier to finagle the truth out of.

Erick stared at the grass, frowning. "Yeah, he was right here. I was surprised they only closed the club for a day and a half. It seemed wrong that people were just walking over where Ruddy had been lying. Did they even wash the blood off of the green?"

I told him, "Bhagwan watered all the greens as soon as everyone left the next morning. It was warm, so he soaked them."

Ann chuckled and looked down, shaking her head. "He'll water the greens for any reason at all, won't he?"

I added, "The police officers and the forensic people had already been here and gone. I guess the board didn't want to anger members by keeping the course closed any longer than necessary." That seemed so self-serving. "The police forensic technician did a cursory sweep of the area. On those television shows, they do so much more, but that's probably not realistic. I don't know whether I expected the officers to examine the grass with a lice comb or what, but it seems like they took a look around and left."

Pauline was neither frowning nor smiling, just regarding the grass with a blank expression. She moved a little closer to Erick. "You think the forensic guys missed evidence?"

Um.

I tried to think of something to say.

Anything.

I stumbled, "I don't really know. When I came out here

the next morning and talked to the officers, they'd already picked up the knife to take it to the state lab for analysis."

All three of them were staring at me.

Erick asked, "What did they find?"

Sherwood's warnings rose in my mind.

I sucked in a deep breath and said, "Constable Sherwood Kane said that the state lab can take a long time to do the analysis and send back the results."

That was true.

It wasn't the answer to his question, but it was true.

I still felt bad about saying it.

Erick nodded, though he was still staring at the ground where Ruddy's body had lain.

Pauline took a step closer to him, though she also did not look up from the grass.

There was no discernible difference in the grass where Ruddy had been lying. The stems were neither crushed nor had any vibrant growth due to his blood fertilizing the soil. All the grass was perfectly the same, which if anything, made it more horrible.

Ann took a step closer, barely took her stance over her putt, and knocked her ball in the hole. She skirted the area where Ruddy's body had been to retrieve her ball. "Let's just putt out and move on."

Erick said, "I've only got six inches left. That's a gimme."

Ann said, "There are no gimmes in Ladies' League."

He took an awkward stance, keeping his toes away from the area where Ruddy's body had been. "You ladies are tough. In the men's league, anything under three feet or so is a gimme."

Yes, well, women play by the rules, which is why women's sports are purer than men's sports. Men flop all over the place during games, pretending to be fouled to make the refs call a yellow card or get a free shot. Women play sports as they were intended.

I tapped my ball in for a bogey, and so did Pauline.

Getting away from the seventeenth green seemed like the most important thing right now. I didn't want to hang out there even a second longer. I don't believe in ghosts and I don't believe in haunted things, but jeez, it felt weird to stand where Ruddy's corpse had been lying on the ground.

I trotted over to where we had left our carts with Ann walking right beside me. We slapped our putters into our bags and left the area as quickly as we could, pushing the heavy carts uphill toward the eighteenth hole, her bright red golf shoes clicking metallically on the asphalt of the cart path.

Behind us, I didn't hear anything.

I didn't hear Pauline and Erick following us and pushing their carts.

I glanced back to where Pauline and Erick were still standing on the seventeenth green, staring at the scene where the murder had taken place.

Pauline reached out and caught Erick's fingers in hers.

A Murder at the Country Club

Erick tugged her close to his side and wrapped his arm around her waist, dropping a quick kiss on her temple just under the brim of her hat.

I turned and faced the eighteenth, pushing my cart directly down the cart path.

Pauline Damir had been married to her husband, Tom, for over twenty years. I had taught their kids in kindergarten. There had been no rumblings on the golf grapevine that they were separated or getting a divorce.

And I could say exactly the same thing about Erick Walters. His wife had mentioned that they were going to Europe that fall for a river cruise.

Such things happened around country clubs. People were thrown together on boards or in foursomes, and sometimes attractions turned into affairs.

But I had never heard a whisper about Pauline and Erick.

And yet, there they were.

And Erick's quick move to grab the knife that had killed Ruddy Agani that first night suddenly made much more sense. If he had already known that Ruddy was dead, he might have decided to wipe her fingerprints off the knife or smudge them enough so that they were unusable.

Pauline had been drunk at the reception after the glow-ball tournament, as if she had been upset and thrown back a few drinks to calm herself.

She would have had plenty of time to tell Erick what had

happened before the four of us walked out to look for Ruddy.

"Hey, Bee! You walked right past the eighteenth tee box!" Ann yelled from behind me.

I stopped, my golf shoes skidding on the loose gravel. "Oops."

I backed up along the cart path, not turning around to see where Pauline and Erick were.

"You okay? Ann asked. "Something bothering you?"

And now I needed another lie. "I'm just really concerned about the club," I said. "Just barely enough people finally signed up for the Nine and Dine this Friday. There's just a lot of preparation to do to for it, and I'm not sure how I'm going to pull it all together."

Ann exclaimed, "I can help out! Why didn't you say something, Bee? I can do whatever you need help with."

And now my lie had turned into something I had to deal with. "I would appreciate it if you could be here Friday at three o'clock to help me decorate for the Nine and Dine."

Ann grinned at me. "You bet."

CHAPTER 26

AFTER WE ALL completed our nine holes of golf, I dismissed Ladies' League and trudged into the clubhouse to have lunch with Trudi. At least our lunch would be a bright spot in my day. Finding out that Erick and Pauline were probably having an affair had messed with my head to the point where I didn't know which direction was up anymore.

As I climbed the stairs from the ladies' locker room in the basement up to the clubhouse's dining room, I saw that Trudi was already sitting at a table and perusing the menu as if she had never seen it before.

Trudi was not a creature of habit. Trudi might order anything at all off the menu and did not play favorites, except for her once-monthly BLT, as allowed by her cardiologist.

I collapsed into the seat across from her. Chilly air from the air conditioner sprayed over the room and drew a line down the back of my neck. "You would not believe what happened at Ladies' League today."

And yet, I realized to my horror that I couldn't tell her what had happened at Ladies' League.

In the dining room, all the ladies who had been out on the golf course that morning for league were sitting around us, ordering their lunch. Discussing the murder with Trudi right here, in the middle of Canterbury Golf Club, was completely impossible.

Everyone would hear.

Everyone would *talk*.

The murderer would either hear that we suspected them or would know that we didn't, if we were completely wrong in all our theories.

Trudi didn't look up from her menu. "Oh? Did you almost get that elusive hole-in-one again? Did the ball roll up to the hole and somehow manage not to fall in *again?*"

"Uh, yeah?"

Trudi lowered her menu slightly, just enough to peer over the top of it with one eyebrow raised at me. "I assume we'll discuss that later, too."

Oh, she had already figured out that we shouldn't discuss my suspicions in public.

I pulled my cell phone out of my pocket. "I just have to get this."

Trudi glared at me over her menu with that suspicious eyebrow waggling at me, again. She knew that my phone had neither buzzed nor chimed.

A Murder at the Country Club

I pulled Trudi's contact up and texted to her, *Pauline Damir and Erick Walters are having an affair. It's possible that he picked up the knife that night to obscure her fingerprints or his own on it.* I tapped the screen and sent the text.

Trudi's purse rattled against the back of her chair, but she ignored it because the waitress was there to take our order. Trudi said, "I'll have the summer salad with grilled chicken, please. Extra grapes."

As I ordered a club sandwich with tomato soup, Trudi reached around the back of her chair to retrieve her phone, glanced at it, and tucked it back in her purse. When the waitress left, Trudi said, "I'm going to the ladies' locker room."

Uh oh. "Trudi, what are you doing?"

"You stay here. I'll be back in just a few minutes." She picked up her purse.

Trudi had been a scientist before she retired, and she kept all kinds of things in that enormous carpetbag of hers. I warned her, "Trudi."

"If that's the case, we should just take a little look around." She glanced around the dining room, where every table had four or more ladies seated, all of them lunching happily. "After all, if everyone's here, the locker room would be the place to be."

She stood, slinging her massive beast of a purse over her shoulder, and walked toward the stairs.

"Trudi!" I jumped up and ran after her, assuring the

waitress along the way that we would be right back and to leave our lunches on the table. "You shouldn't—*and wait for me!*"

Trudi beat me down the stairs to the busy hallway and the women's locker room because although she had short legs, that little woman could scamper like a squirrel. She dodged between all the people walking between the pro shop and the locker rooms like a sprite slipping between willow trees.

I slapped open the door that had just barely closed. "Whatever are you—*oh my heavens and angels.*"

Trudi was on her knees with her purse in front of the lower locker that was embossed with the nametag for Pauline Damir. Small, silver tools were scattered on the floor beside her.

Other than Trudi, the entire locker room was empty of people.

She said, "Look, if we suspect that Pauline might have murdered Ruddy and/or Lale Kollen, then she is somewhat of a threat to everybody at the club. I don't like that you were out there on the golf course all morning with her if she might be dangerous. We need to know whether she did it, and if we find anything like blood on her golf clothes or shoes or whatever, we will turn it over to the police."

"But how shall we say we got that evidence? Don't you need a search warrant or something?" I asked her.

"Nah, I'm on the clubhouse committee. Our bylaws say

that any area of the clubhouse can be searched at any time. It was mostly to keep people from hiding cocaine in the lockers, but I'm sure it would apply to murder weapons, too. By the way, the other day at the club board meeting, Erick Walters said that he wanted me to look at some spreadsheets."

I told her, "We have the murder weapon. It's a knife. It was lying on the ground next to Ruddy with his blood on it. The murder weapon is not the problem. I don't think we should be searching people's lockers."

"Then we are looking for other evidence. I'm not saying that Pauline killed someone else, but the chances are higher, statistically, for somebody who has already killed someone to do it again."

I fretted, "This feels wrong. Shouldn't we at least get a master key or something?"

Trudi picked up one of the small silver implements beside her knee. "I just happen to have some little probes and needles in my purse. You never know when these kinds of things will come in handy. And these locks on these lockers are about thirty years old and about as secure as the lock on my bathroom door, which my cat can unlock." She inserted a silver wire into the lock and another thing that looked like a mini-crochet hook right above it.

"Should I even ask how you know how to pick locks?"

"You pick up a lot of skills being a professor," Trudi muttered as she manipulated the small tools. "Graduate students locked their lab keys in their desk drawers all the time, and it was just easier to get them out this way than it was to call the custodian or campus security. Plus, sometimes you have to make sure that no one is taking the reagents home for more nefarious purposes."

I was shocked. "Did some of your graduate students make drugs for tuition money?"

"Drugs, no. Glitter bombs to torture each other, yes. Those kids were weird. And there it is." She sat back. The locker door swung open.

I bent to peer inside the locker. "We shouldn't be doing this."

"And yet, you have not left in protest." Trudi reached inside the locker and pulled out a few items. "Shampoo, conditioner, basic makeup kit. Her golf shoes are in here, but they're clean." The turned them over. "But there's a bit of mud and grass on the bottom. It doesn't look like she washed them to try to hide blood anytime recently."

"I still can't believe she's having an affair with Erick Walters," I said.

Trudi shrugged. "That's not what we care about here. Besides, affairs aren't shocking."

I sat back on my heels and looked at my friend of thirty years. "Trudi, did you have an affair?"

She shook her head dismissively and frowned. "No, but I worked in a university department. There's a lot of hormones going around with those young twenty-year-olds.

A Murder at the Country Club

You see things that maybe you wish you hadn't. Let's say that I don't find affairs between anybody shocking."

"Do you see anything in Pauline's locker that would suggest she killed Ruddy?"

"No. This was just a waste of time." Trudi rearranged everything in the locker just as we had found it and slammed the door with a clank. "Anybody else you want to check up on while we're breaking into lockers?"

"I feel guilty enough about this already, and we didn't find anything. We can't just open everybody's locker and see if we find something."

Trudi mused, "That's not a bad idea."

"It's not a good one, either. Clubs like this are run on trust. If it gets out that we've been breaking into lockers to try to figure out who the murderer is, people wouldn't like it. We've lost enough members as it is."

Trudi plucked a tissue from the box on the counter and wiped off her small tools. "Still, it's better than letting a murderer hang out around the club, especially when we have late events like that Nine and Dine, coming up."

I climbed to my feet, and Trudi walked over to throw away the tissues. She stepped on the pedal to open the top of the trashcan and was holding her hand suspended over it when she said, "Well, what do we have here?"

"We have something?" I came and stood beside her and looked in the trashcan.

Inside, a white leather golf glove was half-hidden by

213

paper towels. From what parts of it that we could see, brown stained the thumb and first finger.

I asked, "What? Somebody threw away a muddy glove?"

Trudi shook her head. "I don't think that's mud."

"Oh, my word. We found a bloody glove, of all things." I squinted and peered at it more closely. "I think it looks like mud."

"Of course, the blood has dried. It was over a week ago. Or even if it's Lale's blood, it's been a few days. But that doesn't look like mud. The splash material itself is too thin. There are streaks and sprays. It's not clumpy or grainy, and there are no specks in it like you would expect to find if it were dirt."

"Bhagwan does overwater the course. It could be thin mud or thick pond water."

"It might not be."

"If we think it might be blood, we should just hand it over to the police."

"If it is just mud, then we look stupid, especially when I can just test it and see if it is blood."

I frowned at her. "Do you still have lab privileges at the university?"

Trudi laughed. "I don't need a lab. I just need the first-aid kit."

"Oh, Trudi, I don't think we should do this." I rummaged under the sink to find the first-aid kit. "What do you need?"

A Murder at the Country Club

"Rubbing alcohol, a cotton swab, and hydrogen peroxide." She produced a small bottle from her purse.

I got two paper towels from the dispenser and carefully fished the brown-stained glove out of the trash, holding it away from myself in the paper towels.

Trudi said, "Lay it on the countertop."

I did, carefully avoiding any little water spots that might have still been on the counter.

The brown stuff might be mud.

I really hoped the brown stuff was mud.

Trudi opened the bottle of rubbing alcohol and moistened the cotton swab with the astringent liquid. The smell of a hospital lingered in the air of the locker room.

I asked, "How are we going to explain to the police that some of the blood is missing, if it even is blood?"

"We will tell them that we have no idea how that little bit went missing, and they probably won't even notice, anyway. Forensic technicians aren't real scientists." She gently brushed the damp swab over the edge of one of the glove's fingers, where the brown stain was the darkest. She rubbed the leather glove until the cotton was faintly brown.

Trudi opened a tiny vial that she had retrieved from her purse and squeezed one drop of the solution onto the tip of the cotton swab. "This is phenolphthalein."

"What on Earth is that?" I asked her, squinting and trying to read the label without my readers. "It looks like it has too many consonants."

"A very useful reagent. Not only is it one of the principal reagents in the Kastle-Meyer Test for blood that we are currently performing, but it's also a really useful pH indicator for other assays, not to mention a powerful laxative if someone makes me angry."

Trudi scared me sometimes. "You wouldn't put that in someone's food, would you?"

She glanced at me and went back to staring at the cotton swab. "Of course not. I would never do such a thing."

She had been my closest friend since our college days when the dorm lottery had assigned us to be roommates. "What did you do?"

Trudi grimaced and stared at the ceiling for a second. "Remember when those guys were grabbing at the women last year? And then there was a rumor that the really horrible stomach flu that was also going around was transmitted by grabbing women's boobs?"

"You didn't!"

"That's exactly my story, that I didn't do it. And now we put the hydrogen peroxide on and see if it turns pink."

Trudi gently dripped just a little hydrogen peroxide on the swab.

Even without my readers, I could see that the beige-stained cotton turned quite pink.

Trudi sighed. "That means it's positive for blood. That glove is covered with blood. I admit, I was hoping it was just mud, too."

"We'll have to give it to the police."

"Of course, just as soon as we figure out whose glove it is."

"I'm calling them right now." I grabbed my phone out of my pocket.

Trudi looked pensively at the glove lying among the paper towels. "Almost assuredly, a woman put it in this trash can. That hallway outside the door always has people walking down it. If a man had come into the women's locker room, all heck would've broken loose. Therefore, we can assume in the absence of any broken-loose heck, that a woman must have been in the locker room and put it in the trash."

My phone rang the police station, and I waited for them to answer. "Trudi, let the police handle it."

She inserted a slim metal rod inside the glove and lifted the edge, craning her neck to peer inside. "It's a left-handed glove, so the person plays golf right-handed, as seventy-five percent of the club does. That rules out Manpreet, Xun, and Sultana, that I know of. I don't think any of the women play Tommy-two-hand with two gloves."

"Trudi, quit messing with it."

"This glove is made out of Cabretta leather," she continued as she examined it, "not the cheapo synthetic stuff. Sung-Min only wears fabric gloves because her palms sweat too much, but it could be anybody else's. The police aren't going to be able to lift a fingerprint off of that suede surface on the inside. It's seen light use, probably only a few rounds. Someone threw it away because it had blood on it, not because it was worn out."

"Trudi, just stop."

She tilted her head, looking at where she was lifting the edge with the metal probe. "The tag says it's a women's medium, so it would fit around half of the ladies of the club. Not me, of course, but you wear a ladies' medium."

"Don't even bring me into this." I covered my phone's microphone with my hand, even though it was still ringing. "How do you know what size glove I wear?"

Trudi shrugged. "I'm not blind. Besides, you get your weird brand of gloves by the dozen at the sports store in Hamilton when you get your clubs regripped."

"I do not want to know how you know all this stuff about me." And I felt bad that I didn't know the same sort of things about her, as usual.

A voice emerged from the phone in my hand.

"Hello, officer!" I said. "This is Beatrice Yates over at Canterbury Golf Club, where Ruddy Agani was murdered? We found a glove in the trash in the ladies' locker room, and we think you should have a look at it."

I talked to them for a few minutes, giving them the basic details, while Trudi threw the evidence of our little scientific experiment in the Dumpster outside.

Just as she entered the locker room where I was waiting with the bloody glove, two police officers followed her in.

A Murder at the Country Club

Officer Sandy was there again, my ex-student, who made me feel old just by existing as an adult in the world. The other officer introduced herself as Officer Amira Hashami.

As expected, the officers wanted to take possession of the glove, so we backed away from where we had laid it on the counter, still wrapped in paper towels.

Officer Hashami picked it up with tongs and dropped it into a plastic Ziploc bag. She started filling out a label for it.

Officer Sandy turned to me. When she was five, I'd braided her straight, black hair into pigtails because she had gotten too hot from playing on the monkey bars at recess. She asked, "Was there anything else in the trash can?"

Trudi and I glanced at each other, eyes wide.

I said, "I guess we just saw the glove and it looked like it might be blood, so we didn't look any farther."

"Let's take a look." Sandy tipped over the trash can and crouched, sorting through the fluff of paper towels spread over the carpeting by pushing the paper aside with a pen.

As would be expected for a trash can next to a sink in a women's bathroom, a whole lot of damp paper towels flowed out that smelled faintly of the green-and-forest balsam soap in the sink dispensers and the shower stall.

Something thunked out of the trashcan and rolled onto the floor.

"What was that?" Sandy asked and used her pen to poke through the rubbish.

She cleared away the paper towels, revealing two golf

balls.

One was printed in the design of a yellow and black soccer ball.

The other was white with pink hearts scattered over it.

"Hey," Trudi said. "That looks like the one I found in the water hazard and gave you."

"Yeah," I said, frowning. "And the other one looks like my favorite bumblebee-colored soccer ball that went missing last week. I thought it must have dropped out of my bag while I was on the course."

"Did you lose the one with pink hearts?" Officer Sandy asked.

"I don't know. Let me look in my bag."

We went out to my car, and I dug around in the big pocket on my golf bag and the milk crate in the trunk, too. "I don't see it."

Officer Sandy was frowning. "So, think before you tell me this. Is it true that two golf balls that resemble ones that had been in your possession were found in the same trash bag as the glove, which may have blood on it and be linked to the two recent murders?"

"Well, yes," I said, "but I lost them."

Sandy nodded slowly. "I'll make sure to note in the report that you said you lost them, Mrs. Bee. Just between us, please be careful what you tell police officers and, um," she glanced toward the clubhouse, "be careful that no more of your stuff turns up near bloody objects that might be related to a murder, okay?"

After she left, I asked Trudi, "Did she just say that was evidence against me?"

Trudi was frowning. "I wish I'd thought to look deeper in that trash bag. We could have gotten those golf balls out before the police saw them."

CHAPTER 27

THE NEXT MORNING, I was on the driving range at seven o'clock sharp, taking my frustration out on a bucket of golf balls.

Though the morning was warm, a light fog hung over the end of the driving range, near the forest that ringed the country club. The mist scuttled over the grass like ghosts.

I shook my head as I gripped my driver, trying to clear my mind of all thoughts of ghosts, dead people, or murders.

When a car pulled into the small parking lot behind me, I pulled back and whacked the next golf ball as far as I could, which wasn't nearly as far as I would have liked.

Footsteps crunched on the gravel and then were muffled in the grass as someone walked toward me.

I didn't hear the repetitive clink of someone carrying golf clubs in a bag.

I spun, holding my driver at shoulder level so I could knock the intruder's head off with it.

The man walking toward me was Constable Sherwood
Kane, and he was marching over the grass, his arms
swinging at his sides in anger. "What are you doing, talking
to the police and making yourself a bigger suspect than you
already were?"

I said, "I told them the truth. What was I supposed to
do, lie?"

He stood in front of me, his hands opening and closing
like he was trying to figure out what to say. "First, you
'found' one murder victim—"

"Three other people were with me when we discovered
him. I have an alibi for most of the evening." *Most of it.*

"And then you found another murder victim, but you
were all alone that time."

"Other people can account for my whereabouts all
morning."

"Lale Kollen wasn't killed that morning. She was
definitely killed the night before. That's why her porch light
was still on."

"Oh, yeah. I noticed her front yard light was on. But the
fact that I didn't know when she was killed means that I
didn't do it."

"Do you have an alibi for the night before?"

Not anything that anyone could verify. "I was at home,
socializing my foster kittens. You can ask my neighbor,
Coretta Dickinson, whether my lights were on. She was
probably snooping."

A Murder at the Country Club

"So you were alone and have no alibi for the time of the murder, and now you've 'found' a glove with blood all over it."

"Trudi von Shike actually found it, and she's not a suspect at all."

"And two of your golf balls were sitting beside it."

"I told Officer Sandy that I lost those."

"And you were the only other person in the room with Ms. von Shike, your best friend, who backs up your claim that she found the glove just like any best friend would."

"Half the female population of the Canterbury Golf Club had been in that locker room in the last few hours. It was Ladies' League day. Besides, I'm not even the best suspect for Ruddy's murder. Oliver Shwetz had just had an argument with him. Plus, Ruddy's wife, Linda, was getting ready to divorce him. They'd just had a huge fight that night. She'd already made plans to move to California."

Sherwood shook his head. "Linda Agani has an ironclad alibi for Ruddy's murder and a gambling problem. We talked to her about her whereabouts that night. They had that argument about four o'clock that afternoon, before Ruddy showed up at the golf club for the outing. Right after their argument, she left the house and went to the tribal casino about twenty miles away."

"Well, that's what she *says* she did," I countered.

"The casino's closed-circuit security cameras show her car driving into the parking garage and a woman matching her description walking into the casino. Her slots reward card was in use in various slot machines for seven hours, and we can track a woman who looks just like her walking around the casino on the closed-circuit cameras. Her movements match the location of her slots reward card, too."

"Maybe she had a friend drive her car to fake an alibi," I said, as if I knew anything at all about alibis.

Sherwood said, "We asked around the casino, and some of the other regulars know her and said that she was there that night. She even ran a red light near the casino on her way home, and a red-light camera took a picture that shows her license plate, her car, and her face at three in the morning, well after the murder. Linda Agani didn't do it, and we would be laughed out of court if we charged her. It's about as close to an ironclad alibi as you can get. She couldn't have set that alibi up any tighter if she had tried."

I put my driver back into my bag and pulled out a shorter iron. "She's not the only suspect. Trudi and I have been trying to figure out who killed Ruddy. Considering that Lale Kollen was going to inherit Ruddy's estate, maybe you should look at who gets the money now."

"Please, for the love of all that is holy, *stop*. You're making yourself look worse and worse. It's not that we don't want your help. It's just that you are making yourself look like the most likely suspect every time you find something. Please, Bee, stop snooping around with this. If for no other reason, the person who killed Ruddy may have thought that

Lale Kollen was getting too close to figuring out that they did it, and that's why they killed her, too."

"You keep suggesting that one person killed both of them," I said.

He sighed. "Because we've had two related murders involving knives in the last few weeks, the crime lab expedited our evidence. The same unknown fingerprints that were on the knife that killed Ruddy was also on the knife that killed Lale Kollen. It looks like the same person committed both murders. Ruddy was killed with two stab wounds. One hit a rib and bounced off. The second one hit his aorta, and it blew up. Lale Kollen had three stab wounds. One found her left ventricle. That knife was most likely from Lale's knife rack, right there in the house. It matched her knife set and had her fingerprints on it, too."

"If you'll just listen to me," I said. "If you'll just let me tell you what we found out about Pauline Damir—"

He held up his hands. "Don't say anything else. If you tell me something, then I have to tell the police what you said and that you told it to me. It will put you in an even worse situation."

I begged him, *"Just listen to me."*

Sherwood pressed his hands over his ears. "I am leaving. Don't tell me anything."

He walked back to his car, and I was shaking so badly that I couldn't hit any more golf balls.

CHAPTER 28

THE NEXT AFTERNOON, the dining room in CGC's clubhouse was arranged just as it always was for everyday use. Crisp, white tablecloths draped gracefully over square tables set for four or longer tables for eight people. Low centerpieces of silk flowers and golf pencils stood in the centers. Comfortable, upholstered armchairs ringed every table. The entire clubhouse was decorated in navy blue, gold, and white, typical New England colors. The ceiling soared above, nearly three stories above my head. At the end of the dining room, a glass wall of windows let the afternoon light shine in. The dining room could hold about a hundred people comfortably, or a hundred and fifty if we used stand-up serving stations.

Only sixty people had signed up for the Nine and Dine this sultry Friday night, so we didn't have to lift the wings of the square tables to turn them into round tables that could seat six or even eight people, in a pinch. I had about two hours to whip this dining room into a fun and interesting party space.

Usually, I could count on at least a hundred people to sign up for the Nine and Dine, a regularly scheduled event that takes place on the second Friday evening of every month. After a fun nine-hole golf scramble, everybody came into the clubhouse's dining room for a sit-down New England supper. Sometimes, we served lobster. More often, supper was scallops, seafood, and steaks.

But as always for the Nine and Dine, the dining room needed to be decorated in a festive manner to make sure that people remembered that the social events were one of the benefits of belonging to a club rather than just paying green fees every time they wanted to play a round of golf.

I wasn't feeling particularly festive.

Because we only had a little more than half of our usual sign-ups, Chef Leopold had decided to seize this chance to prepare a more involved menu than usual, probably in the hopes of increasing next month's turnout when word got around about how extravagant the meal had been. Every table was already set with a gold charger for under the plate and an extensive array of silverware, plus two wine glasses.

With all those forks lined up and shining in the afternoon sunlight, it looked like Chef Leo was going to serve at least five courses.

He was going over the top for just a Nine and Dine. This wasn't the Winter Formal or the Halloween Devil's Ball, a pun related to how people complained that their golf balls must be possessed, and that's why the balls didn't fly or land as the person had intended.

I was glaring at the dining room, my fists braced on my hips, as I tried to figure out how to decorate this little clubhouse using no additional money because the club was insolvent.

Behind me, a woman's voice said, "Hi, Bee. What do you need help with?"

A thousand things ran through my head that I needed help with, starting with figuring out how to convince the police that I was not the number-one suspect in the murders of Ruddy Agani and Lale Kollen.

However, I turned and beamed at her. "Hello, Ann! We need to decorate for tonight's after-golf supper. I've done this so many times that I don't have any ideas left."

Ann Carmo smiled, her crimson lips curving upward. You never caught Ann without her lipstick and earrings. She said, "We can narrow it down. When you are buying a boat, there are three things to think about: speed, comfort, and cost. You can have any two of those you want, but no one can have all three. You can have comfort and cost, but it's going to be a slow boat with a small motor. Or you can have speed and comfort, but that's going to cost you. So, you have to ask yourself, which two things are the most important here?"

I scratched my head. "I'm sorry, Ann. It's been a rough

couple of weeks for me. I don't get what you're trying to say."

"Basically, I'm saying that we may need to do this cheaply, easily, and quickly, but you can only have two of those. The only way to get it done easily and quickly would be to hire someone else to do it, and that would mean it wouldn't be done cheaply. If you want to do it cheaply and easily, we might have to find some things at our houses or call a bunch of people to see what they have, which means that it wouldn't be done quickly. See? You have to choose your priorities."

I mused, "I think it should be done cheaply and quickly, which according to your rubric, means that it can't be done easily, right?"

"Right. That means we're going to have to put in some sweat equity and figure out how to do things the smart way. So, are there any decorations, maybe some hiding in the clubhouse or in your garage, that we can re-purpose for tonight's Nine and Dine?"

I thought so hard that my eyes rolled up in my head, mentally ransacking the club. "That narrows things down a bit. I gave away most of my holiday decorations when I downsized to my little cottage, but there is a storeroom here at the clubhouse that we can look at. I don't think anybody's even been in there for ten years."

Ann Carmo's face lit up in a grin. "Oh, I love poking around secret places. Let's go."

A Murder at the Country Club

I led her down the stairs, past the ladies' locker room, to a rarely used door at the end of one of the hallways. I pulled out my little keychain, and thanks to Ruddy's thrifty ways, the key to my office door fit the lock to the door of the storeroom, too.

Inside, I flipped on the light switch. Dust floated in the glow from the fluorescent tube lights overhead. Brown boxes were stacked against one wall, while plastic storage containers in crayon colors filled the other side of the room.

I walked inside and surveyed the boxes.

Masking tape labels striped most of the boxes' lids. Blocky letters spelled out the names of holidays and themes, like Fourth of July, Christmas Ball, Kentucky Derby, and America's Cup Party.

"Carrying this stuff upstairs is going to be difficult," Ann said. "But, if we use something from down here, it will be cheap and quick."

I walked around the boxes, trailing my fingers over the gritty lids. "Christmas in May?"

"Oh! These decorations for the America's Cup would be nautical and New England-ish. Isn't Chef Leo serving a seafood platter for dinner?"

"Yeah, we could just put these out and be done with it. Help me carry this box upstairs."

With some huffing and puffing, the two of us managed to wrestle the long, heavy bin up the stairs and to the dining room. It wasn't easy.

Inside, we found adorable, wooden sailboats, navy blue chair bunting, and some prints of sailboats that we could insert in the frames instead of our usual paintings.

Ann rubbed her hands together. "If you'll start on the pictures, I'll run around and decorate. Shouldn't take too long."

Indeed, I found a screwdriver and started taking apart the picture frames for the rather nice prints of yachts cresting teal ocean waves.

Ann bustled around the dining room, her arms full of little wooden ships, and she put together new centerpieces on the tables that, somehow, looked nothing like the original golf-themed ones, even though many of the elements were the same. She collected all the cups of golf pencils in the plastic bin and began tying the navy-blue fabric around the backs of the chairs.

I managed to get two of the prints put into frames in fifteen minutes. "This isn't going to take long at all. We'll have you out of here in an hour or so."

Ann was leaning over the place settings at a long table, fussing over some silk greenery to integrate a tiny sailboat into the centerpiece. "I don't have anywhere to go. I suppose I could go home and shower before the event, but we are playing nine holes of golf, first."

"Oh, I didn't know you were coming to the Nine and Dine tonight." With all the distractions lately, I'd just looked at the total number of people and hadn't taken a close look at the sign-up sheet.

"Oh, yes. I like to participate in the social events here at the club. I think Sherlynne paired me with the Nagarkars and Mint Bunnag for the scramble."

"Isn't your husband signed up?" I asked as I used a screwdriver to pry a tough staple loose from the wooden picture frame.

Ann laughed. "No, Wilber doesn't do social stuff like this very often."

"But he golfs, doesn't he?" I asked her. There wasn't much point of paying for a CGC family membership unless at least two people golfed at least some. A single membership would be cheaper. I was just looking to save her some money.

"Oh, yes, but not enough, and not well. His idea of a sport is sitting in the sun and waiting for a fish to eat his bait."

I laughed. "Ah, he's big into fishing, then."

"Not so much anymore."

I sat back on my heels. "Hey, can I ask you something?"

"We've known each other for decades. I can't imagine what you don't know already."

I gestured with my screwdriver toward the golf course beyond the windows. "Are you okay after we found Ruddy, out there?"

Ann had moved from making the centerpieces to decorating the chairs at the long table, and she paused as she was tying a bow in the dark-blue bunting. "It was weird. I won't pretend it wasn't weird. I spontaneously said yes when you said you needed people to look for Ruddy. And then I found myself traipsing all over the golf course in high heels, and we found him. I'm still kind of shocked about how everything happened that night."

"Yeah, I was surprised that you didn't change into your golf shoes like Trudi and Erick did."

"They were already in my car. It would have taken too long to go get them."

"How well do you know Pauline Damir?" I asked, pretending to be very busy with the picture frame.

Ann stood and progressed to the next table, picking out a little anchor and a sailor to tuck into the centerpiece. "Not that well. I mean, she's been around. We've been members here at Canterbury for several years, but I've only been active here in the past year or so. I'm just getting to know a lot of the people here."

"Yeah, but you've lived in the town of Canterbury for a long time, even back before you had your kids."

She brushed the wine glasses at one of the place settings as she reached for the centerpiece, and the crystal glasses rang together. "After I quit working for the school and had my kids, I just knew other mommies for a long time."

This happened to a lot of women. Not to me, obviously, though I certainly knew the mommy crowd from having been the town's kinder teacher. "So you don't know Pauline that well."

"Not really. She's the florist who was talking at Ladies' League about how Ruddy had been messing up her business by not paying her, right?"

"She mentioned that. She was hanging around with you at the reception after the glow-ball tournament that night, right?"

"She and I played with Arnie Holmes that night. She was already wasted by the time you asked people to go with you to look for Ruddy. I didn't know she drank that much."

Yes, the two of them had played with my Uncle Arnie that night. As a matter of fact, my uncle Arnie's group had just been finishing up and coming inside when Ruddy and Oliver Shwetz had been arguing. Ruddy had almost bowled Pauline over when he'd stomped out of the clubhouse.

I asked Ann, "After you came in, did Pauline stick to you the whole night? Do you think that there may have been some time, maybe half an hour or so, maybe a little bit after Ruddy stormed out of the clubhouse, that you didn't see her for a while?"

Ann turned and looked right at me. "Yeah, there was. We had played together, so it's an unwritten rule that you're supposed to hang out together, afterward. You know, because it mixes up the couples so we don't have ironclad cliques forming."

"Yeah, it's one of the reasons we hold so many of these social events like scrambles with assigned teams, to mix everybody up."

"Anyway, I was hanging out with Arnie in the bar, drinking for a while, and then I came out to get a fresh plate of hors d'oeuvres. That was when I found Pauline again, and she was already half-soused. I don't know where she'd been for the previous hour or so."

"So there's an hour missing from Pauline's alibi," I mused.

"Alibi?" Ann gasped. "Do you think *Pauline Damir* killed Ruddy Agani?"

I went back to smoothing a print into the picture frame. "Someone did."

"I still don't think a woman could have done it. It would have taken a big man to kill someone like Ruddy Agani. Do you know where Oliver Shwetz was the whole night? He had that argument with Ruddy."

"I told Oliver he could go up to my office to calm down, and then I didn't see him for the rest of the night. I think he went home."

Ann shook her head, her dark ponytail twitching. "I wouldn't believe a word Oliver Shwetz said about anything. I've heard that he was involved in a lot of shady deals over at the Gnostic Yacht Club, too, and I wonder if Ruddy found out about them. Maybe that's why they were arguing, and maybe that's why Oliver killed him."

I glanced at Ann. "I didn't know Oliver was a member over at the Gnostic."

"Oh, yes," she nodded while she was tying the blue chair bunting in a neat bow. "Oliver was a big sailor, and he was very involved in their finances. He was on the board and had the power to write checks."

Oliver must not have been concerned with having to sue the yacht club. "He wasn't involved in their embezzlement scandal, though."

"They never caught who did it. They just closed the club."

"That's odd," I said.

Ann shrugged. "Canterbury is a small town. Things happen, and people who have friends don't get charged with things. Oliver is close friends with the chief of police and the mayor."

Those weird spreadsheets I'd found disturbed me even more. "The Canterbury police chief and mayor are members here, too."

"Hmmm," Ann said. "And so is Oliver Shwetz, and the club has cash flow problems. That's odd, isn't it?"

When I looked over, Ann was staring straight at me, her eyebrows raised.

"Yeah," I said, nodding and unhappy. "It's odd."

After Ann left, I took one last look around the clubhouse that was now ready for the Nine and Dine.

The centerpieces were cozy and cute. The pictures were now nautical and sporty, rather than golfy and sporty. The chair backs were festooned with navy-blue bunting.

However—

Some of the place settings were wrong.

I walked among the tables, examining them.

One plate at a four-person table had no dessert fork across the top.

Another plate at a table by the window was missing both its soup and coffee spoons.

All the settings at a long table near the back were missing their knives.

I went back to the kitchen to tell Leopold that the tables needed to be checked for silverware, and he blew up at me that all the tables, *all of them*, were perfect, and how could I talk about silverware at a time like this? He went back to standing over a bubbling pot that smelled like browning butter and garlic.

I grabbed Melanie, the hostess, and alerted her about the silverware problem. She sighed and said she would take care of it. "I set those utensils out with the girls. We set each one individually. I walked around with all the main course knives and placed them at each setting, and Jennie gave everyone a salad fork, and we kept doing it. I thought we did it all perfectly, you know? I thought every place setting was complete." Melanie shook her head. "I know the club is short of cash, but I think we're going to have to order some more silverware settings. It seems like they just walk off, especially the knives."

CHAPTER 29

ONCE I HAD finished decorating the clubhouse for the Nine and Dine, I grabbed the bundle of the club's prints that had been in the picture frames and took them out to my car. If I'd left them in the kitchen or storage room, someone would have accidentally crushed them, I was sure.

I juggled the rustling rolls of paper with one hand and opened the back door of my sedan with the other, catching them as they nearly fell onto the hot asphalt. Warm air billowed out of my car, and I hurled the rattling paper onto the back seat.

The rolled prints landed on the newspaper from a couple of days ago, the one where Lale Kollen had written that horrible article about the club, calling it the Canterbury Golf and Murder Club.

May God rest her soul.

Man, that article made me so mad.

Not that I had read it.

And not that I ever was going to read it.

If I read that article, it would just make me even more mad at Lale Kollen and the *Canterbury Tales.*

And Lale Kollen was dead.

It would be terrible to be mad at somebody who was dead. That had to be bad karma or a sin or something.

And I certainly hadn't wanted her or anyone else *dead.* I was getting flustered just thinking about it.

Nope, I definitely should not read that article she'd written. I should pick up that newspaper, walk around the clubhouse, and deposit that trash directly into the dumpster.

Yep, that was what I should do.

I picked up the newspaper.

And opened it, knowing full well that if I read that article, I would work myself into a white-hot rage.

Everybody does stupid things, sometimes.

The first few paragraphs were every bit as sensational as that nasty headline. Lale Kollen had written a hatchet piece.

Well, I had known what the article was going to be before I opened up the newspaper, and now I was committed to reading it.

The Canterbury Golf Club has long been an institution in the town of Canterbury, but its presence is not without controversy. Originally, the club was built on land bought from the town at an alarmingly low price. Nepotism and back-room deals were suggested.

* * *

A Murder at the Country Club

That patently was not true. The club had paid the town what the land had been worth *at the time.* The golf club was situated on a parcel that had been so far out from the town center that everyone had thought it was folly to build anything out there in the midst of the cows and vineyards. As a matter of fact, people had laughed at the Canterbury Golf Club for buying such an out-of-the-way plot that would surely come to no good and probably be overrun with chickens, rabbits, and poison ivy within five years.

The club has come under criticism in the last few years for exceeding the amount of water that has been allotted for its use. The club now hogs in excess of three times the amount of water that it has been slated to use, drawing the water from the town's underground perched aquifer, which is depleting rapidly in these times of changing climate.

Yeah, okay. the board really needed to talk to our greenskeeper about that, again. I mean, the fairways and greens looked nice, but the town had set limits on our water use.

But we were also using rain runoff that we caught in our water hazards. It wasn't *all* new water from the town's wells.

But I could see her point on that one.

After the murder occurred at the Canterbury Golf club nearly two weeks ago, the club resumed its normal operations in less than two days.

* * *

My teeth ground together in my head at the thought of this terrible sub-textual accusation. How dare she insinuate that we didn't care about Ruddy Agani's death?

Although, the course had been closed for only about a day and a half, afterward. I hadn't been particularly comfortable with it, either.

But we had to consider the other members, and the police officers had told us that first afternoon that they had finished their investigation at the site.

The police had told us to open the course.

—Maybe because Canterbury's Chief of Police had had tee times that weekend for out-of-town guests.

Oh, I didn't like that at all.

Despite this reporter's ongoing attempt to learn about how the club was investigating the murder of Ruddy Agani, no one from the club has made an official comment on the record. However, at least one person has noted that they want to keep the club's name out of the newspapers.

The club was not investigating the murder.

The Canterbury *police* were investigating the murder because that was their job.

And yeah, that snide comment probably was directed at me. I hoped the rest of the board hadn't given her any comments, either.

Other members of the club, however, have been more forthcoming

A Murder at the Country Club

with details about the terrible night out on the golf course.

Gosh darn it, I wondered which of the members had been squealing.

It has been widely reported and was personally observed by this reporter that the victim of the horrible murder, Mr. Rudolph Agani, had an altercation earlier in the evening in the clubhouse with Mr. Oliver Shwetz of Canterbury. Mr. Shwetz is a local attorney who specializes in small claims and local matters. Though Mr. Shwetz was asked for a comment regarding the murder of Rudolph Agani, he had no comment. Indeed, Mr. Shwetz had a rather extreme reaction to this reporter contacting him, citing that he was bound by attorney-client privilege, and that speaking any more would be a breach of ethical and even legal privileges. At that point, Mr. Shwetz sputtered and devolved into a tirade, railing at this reporter again about attorney-client privilege. This reporter wonders who Mr. Shwetz's client was and what provoked such an extreme reaction to this reporter asking about his involvement.

I lowered the newspaper and looked out over the parking lot.

Oliver had told me that the club had never been one of his clients. It was that whole conflict of interest thing, in case he needed to sue the club.

After what Ann had said, this was just weird.

Dang, I thought newspapers were supposed to answer questions, not make me think up more of them.

Jessa Archer

* * *

Four people went out onto the course that night and discovered the poor, mutilated corpse of Ruddy Agani.

Oh, good grief. Ruddy hadn't been mutilated. Two stabs and nicking the aorta did not add up to "mutilated."

One of the people who found the victim, Ann Carmo, agreed to talk to me about that terrible night.

Huh. Ann hadn't mentioned that she'd talked to Lale Kollen. I hadn't directly asked Ann whether she had spoken to the reporter, but maybe Ann should have told me that she had contacted the other murder victim, too.

Ann Carmo told this reporter that she was horrified at finding the murder victim at the golf course. "Of course, after that explosive argument Ruddy Agani had with Oliver Shwetz in front of everybody, and then when Oliver went missing right afterward, I think we all know what happened. Oliver Shwetz has always had a terrible temper. When he was my lawyer, I was always a little frightened of him."

Oliver didn't have a terrible temper. Ruddy had had a terrible temper, but not Oliver.

Maybe Lale had gotten the names mixed up.

But when we had been talking just a while ago, Ann had mentioned that Oliver had been a member of the Gnostic

246

A Murder at the Country Club

Yacht Club.

But she had said that her husband had been very into sailing and fishing.

If Ann and her husband had belonged to the Gnostic Yacht Club, wouldn't she have said something while we were talking about it?

Because it seemed like she had deliberately not mentioned her own involvement with the yacht club, but she'd specifically pointed out that Oliver was a member.

Discomfort grew in my heart.

And yet, while I was getting very uneasy about Ann and embezzlement, I knew that she couldn't have been the murderer because Ann had worked for the school district with me. Her fingerprints would have been on file with the police for those background checks we did. If Ann had done it, the fingerprints on the knives would have matched hers in the police files.

Another in-depth interview will be published next week in The Canterbury Tales.

This was weird. Only someone who wanted attention would volunteer to be quoted like this. Ann didn't seem like an attention-seeker to me.

But it did seem like someone had been promising to tell Lale Kollen more information about the Canterbury Golf Club and the murder of Ruddy Agani.

What else did Ann know?

I looked around the parking lot, but Ann must have already left the club because her sporty little BMW was gone.

She was supposed to be back for the Nine and Dine that night.

I could ask her about the Gnostic Yacht Club and Oliver Shwetz then.

And I could do that right after I'd finished interrogating Pauline Damir about whether or not she'd killed two people.

Oh, the Nine and Dine was going to be a bundle of laughs tonight.

I flinched, already dreading the confrontation, and walked around to throw the newspaper in the recycling bin behind the clubhouse.

But, of course, as soon as my hand dangled that newspaper with its ugly article over the bin, I snatched it back.

CHAPTER 30

I WALKED BACK into the clubhouse and dumped the offensive newspaper at the end of the bar.

Early-evening sunlight bounced off the polished wood like a laser beam, and I shielded my eyes from the glare, inspecting the two figures in the bar area as I strode over. "Uncle Arnie, my favorite relative! Just the person I wanted to see."

My uncle Arnold Holmes was sipping a pale brown drink in a tall glass, probably an ale of some sort, and he snorted a little of it and coughed as I approached. "Bee, how was your day?"

"*Horrid.* My day has been horrid. My week and my month-to-date have been horrid, thanks to whoever killed Ruddy Agani and now probably Lale Kollen, too."

Uncle Arnie nodded. "That's how it goes."

"What do you know about it?"

Uncle Arnie sighed and set his drink on the bar. "Not

249

too much. If I'd heard anything of value or that I could depend on, I would have called you or told you during one of the times you've driven me to the club."

"Then tell me the gossip. I think I'm missing something, so I need to hear all of it."

"Investigating the murders, are you?"

"Not at all. I just want to know who killed Ruddy and Lale so things can get back to normal."

"Right. That is certainly not investigating." Arnie rotated the tall glass between his palms. Liver spots dappled the backs of his hands. "The primary club gossip is, of course, that you're the murderer."

I raised one finger toward the bartender, who was chopping limes. "Maurice, I'm going to need something strong."

"Now, now, pumpkin," Arnie said. "Has anyone stopped calling you for rides to the club or told you that you shouldn't be in charge of things?"

I considered my ringing phone and packed calendar. "It seems like I've been as busy as ever, driving people over here and seeing to the club's needs."

"I'd say it lends the club and you a bit of mystique. Besides, everyone's willing to risk their life to have you drive them around rather than call an Uber for four bucks."

"They're all cheap bastards." Maurice winked at me as he slid a low drink in front of me. "It's on the house."

"Yeah, you'd better be careful because I'm so

dangerous." I turned back to my uncle. "So, I'm the club's femme fatale."

"Everyone's having fun talking about it, sure." He waggled his white eyebrows at me. "It's *scandalous.*"

I sipped the drink, detecting orange juice, whiskey, and powdered sugar. "Maybe we should incorporate it into the club's advertising."

"Anyway, everyone's talking about it, but no one believes it. So, I don't think you should worry."

I didn't tell him about the mounting evidence against me that the police were accruing. Besides, I knew he was trying to comfort me. The side-eyed reactions at Ladies' League and dwindling interest in social events told me the real story. "What else are they talking about?"

He nodded. "They're talking about the Gnostic Yacht Club a lot."

That was odd. "But it closed. The Gnostic is ancient history."

"Yep, it closed after a bunch of money went missing."

"I know that. Everybody knows that." Well, I knew it after Erick told me, but I didn't gossip much. Other people had probably known about it.

"You know who did it?" my uncle asked me.

I turned on my bar chair and regarded him. "No."

A smug smile creased his face all the way up to the four white hairs stretched across his bright pink scalp. "Nobody does."

"Dang it, Arnie. You got me." I turned back to my drink, which though fruity, was properly strong.

"But I know *how* they did it," he said.

"Now you've got something I should listen to."

"They formed corporations and used them as false vendors. They submitted invoices to the yacht club, and the club paid the invoices."

"But we have better accounting practices than they did," I said, beginning to fret about pages and pages of businesses I'd never heard of written invisibly in white letters on a white spreadsheet.

The companies that Erick had shown me had weird names like Deck Varnish and Rope International. Now that I thought about it, *boats* used deck varnish and rope, not golf courses. If the same people were embezzling here, they hadn't even bothered to change the yacht-based names of the shell companies they'd used.

I was insulted that they thought we were so dumb that we wouldn't notice that a bunch of boat companies were submitting invoices to us.

Even though we hadn't noticed.

"How hard would it be for something like that to happen here?" Arnie asked.

"Completely impossible!" I insisted. "A committee member has to approve each invoice. People have to be elected to committees, and then each committee has to decide which one person will have invoice-approval authority. It could be anybody. Just because you're on a committee doesn't mean you get to approve invoices. And then, after the vendor submits the invoice, and after a specific person on the committee that oversees that particular facet of the club approves it, only then does one of the authorized check-writers like Ruddy cut the check."

"So, it's not like the checks are just lying around for *someone* to tuck up her sleeves like she does the silverware and everyone's personalized golf balls and ball markers. How does a person get on a committee at this club?"

"You have to volunteer to stand for election. You know this."

"Uh-huh, but I'm being Socratic. How many people run for each seat?"

I grimaced. "We never fill all the seats. The vote is a formality."

"Yes, and how does one nominate people for these highly coveted committee positions?"

"We get people drunk and shanghai them while they're smashed."

"Yes, quite. So, if someone were motivated to be part of one of our highly coveted committees, they could volunteer and get one quite easily, right?"

I gripped my cold drink more tightly. "I suppose so."

"How many members serve on committees?"

"We have a dozen or more committees, and each one has between five and fifteen members. The social committee has more than twenty."

"How many committees do you serve on?" he asked.

"Five," I said, not liking where this was going.

"And how about little Trudi?"

"Almost all of them."

"How many members really serve on the committees?"

I thought about it. "Maybe a dozen people fill at least some of the spots on all the committees, and then other people fill the rest of the chairs. But there is always a core of people who keep any organization running. That's normal."

Arnie nodded. "We have a lot of members in common with the now-defunct Gnostic Yacht Club."

Maybe some of the club's revenue shortfall wasn't due to our member-poaching problem, though that was certainly part of it, too. Maybe our expenses were too high because someone was stealing from us.

The first murder victim had been Ruddy Agani, the guy who cut many of the checks that the committees approved, the guy most likely to discover an embezzlement scheme, assuming he hadn't been a part of it.

Or maybe he had delayed payments to the embezzlers like he had everybody else, and they'd gotten mad or scared that they had been found out.

I glanced at the newspaper down at the end of the bar.

And maybe the reporter, Lale Kollen, had found out too much, too.

I tried not to growl, and surely my uncle understood the

anger in my voice. "I need a list."

He said, "You can start with Pauline Damir and her husband."

The Damirs' marriage didn't seem solid enough for them to be partners in crime, and Pauline had mentioned that her flower shop had been in dire straits because Ruddy wasn't paying her. That didn't sound like someone who had a second stream of income from embezzlement.

My suspicions about Pauline lowered a notch, but they didn't go away. "Who else?"

"All the usual suspects about town: the Shirazis, the Sauveterres, the Jacksons, the Walters, Oliver Shwetz, plus the Carmos, Shins, Rinaldis, and Berkowitzes were all members at Gnostic."

"Are those the usual suspects?" I asked, staring into my amber drink.

"They are if we're talking about being members of both clubs."

"Tell me more about the Damirs and the Walters."

"Like what?"

I sipped my drink. The liquor burned my tongue and throat. "Like how long have Pauline and Erick been an item?"

"Ah, so you know about that."

"I suspected."

"Pauline and Erick have only been carrying on for a few months. They were on a committee together."

I swallowed hard. "Which one?"

"Grounds, I think? Or the clubhouse committee?"

"Right." I could find out.

I sipped my drink and asked him about other things, anything to take my mind off of my growing suspicions. "So, what was the final verdict on how people liked the glow-ball tournament, other than the murder on the seventeenth?"

"Oh, people liked it," Uncle Arnie said, signaling to the bartender for another ale.

"Did they, though?" I mused, swirling the dregs of my drink around the ice in my glass. "Sometimes, I think I organize all these things and people only pretend to like them because they're supposed to, but they really don't."

"Oh, no, honey." Arnie wrapped his arm around my shoulders and jostled me around. "People like your events. Ann lost her nifty, glowing ball and wandered around in the dark for an hour looking for it because she's such a magpie, but Pauline and Thorny had a great time. So did everyone else I talked to. You saw that everyone was in high spirits in the clubhouse."

"Yeah." Until Ruddy and Oliver had their spat, but everyone recovered quickly afterward.

"You'll be okay. This murder thing will blow over. Next month, people will be on to something else."

Yeah, they would.

If the murderer were caught.

I needed to talk to Pauline Damir and probably Erick

Walters, too. Maybe I could arrange to sit with Pauline at supper.

The Nine and Dine began in an hour.

Cars were already pulling into the parking lot, and the bag guys were zipping out in their carts to help unload clubs.

CHAPTER 31

THROUGH THE CLUBHOUSE'S front windows, I saw Trudi walking in from the parking lot, so I ran outside to walk in with her.

Other people in the parking lot were farther away than they would be once we all got inside, so people were less likely to overhear us. Plus, people were talking to each other or the bag guys.

"Hey, do you know which committees Pauline Damir is on?" I asked Trudi.

"Pauline?" Trudi scrunched up her face. "I'd have to check the computer, but I thought she resigned from the social committee a few months ago due to time conflicts. I don't think she has any official duties at all right now."

"So, she's not on *any* committees? How did we miss her?"

"I don't know," Trudi mused. "Well, she drinks. We can pour a few down her tonight and put her on the promo committee. That one needs members."

That halfway ruled Pauline out for being part of the embezzlement scheme. She was looking less and less likely to me, and yet, she'd had so much to say about Ruddy. A tickling suspicion about her would not go away. "That's not quite what I mean."

I glanced around the parking lot, but everyone was beyond the median planted with blue hydrangeas.

Ann Carmo zipped her little car into the parking lot and waved to us as she trotted into the clubhouse. We waved back.

When Ann was far enough away, I whispered to Trudi, "It seems that we've had a little embezzlement problem."

"*What!*"

People across the parking lot turned and looked at us, including Pauline Damir and her husband, Tom.

Oliver Shwetz and his wife hurried past them.

Huh, Oliver was showing his face around the club. He must have bought the tickets some time ago.

I laughed and waved at all of them.

They resumed walking in.

"Keep your voice down," I shushed Trudi. "Remember when Erick Walters was talking about spreadsheets in the budget committee meeting a while ago?"

"Sure," she said, her voice rising.

I squinted at her. "Do you really?"

Trudi waved her hand. "I remember that he was holding

a bunch of paper that was probably going to take hours, and I had to get home to my grandbaby."

"Yep, that's the time. Anyway, Erick showed them to me. It didn't click at the time, but some of the companies' names were things like Deck Varnish LLC, Rope International, and Shipmo Corp."

She frowned and gestured toward the clubhouse. "Our deck is concrete. It gets power-washed. What's a shipmo?"

"I know, but *boats* use deck varnish and rope. That's the point. I think whoever embezzled so much from the Gnostic Yacht Club that they had to close—"

Trudi's eyes widened. *"What?"*

More people turned, including Priscilla Sauveterre and her husband, who were walking past a row of sports cars.

Oh, sweet baby-child in a manger, the Sauveterres had been members of the Gnostic.

I laughed and waved again, and I shushed Trudi harder. "People are going to talk."

"You need to tell me what's going on *right now."*

"Someone was embezzling from the Gnostic Yacht Club using shell companies. I think we have a problem, too. I think Erick found some of them on those weird spreadsheets I showed you."

"The spreadsheets with Oliver Shwetz's name on them," Trudi said. "The ones you showed me over lunch."

I stepped back, shocked. I had forgotten that Oliver's name was on them, but it was. That was why Trudi and I had played golf with him and asked him about his clients. That was why he'd gotten mad. "Yes, those spreadsheets."

Trudi asked, "Does Erick Walters still have those spreadsheets? Is he going to be here tonight?"

I gestured toward the winding road that led to Canterbury Vineyard and Winery. "He just drove into the parking lot."

She shook her head. "Dang, but we have a problem."

"And I think everybody who might be involved is coming to the Nine and Dine tonight."

"Oh, lovely. Did we invite a reporter to write it all up for the newspaper?"

I rolled my eyes. "Inviting the media is part of our basic promo effort. They never used to come."

Trudi sighed, "But *all* of them are definitely going to accept their invitations to the Canterbury Golf and Murder Club."

CHAPTER 32

TRUDI WALKED INTO the clubhouse in front of me and scanned the room, looking for who she should talk to during the pre-golf social hour.

I dawdled, ordered a drink from Maurice, and sidled up to Pauline Damir, who was standing near the punchbowl with her husband.

Time to knock at least one suspect off my list of potential murderers.

But I couldn't ask Pauline directly whether she'd killed Ruddy. She would say no, whether she had done it or not. I needed to get Pauline to admit that she was somewhere else during the time that Ann Carmo had said she was unaccounted for. Then, we could determine where Pauline had been, either somewhere innocent or out on the golf course, murdering Ruddy.

Her whereabouts for the time when Lale Kollen had been killed might be of interest, too.

"Hello, Tom and Pauline!" I said, gesturing with a glass of sweet orange-juice stuff and whiskey toward Pauline and her husband. "How are you two doing tonight?"

I chatted with them a while, not insinuating anything at all until Tom went to the bar to procure some before-golf drinks for himself and Pauline.

I turned to her and tilted my head. "Hey, I was wondering, what do you know about Erick Walters?"

Pauline finished sipping her bright pink punch quite deliberately before she said, "I'm not sure what you mean."

I looked up at the corners of the clubhouse's ceiling, where the white molding met the peaked roof, and said, "It seems that he was missing for a while after the glow-ball tournament when everyone else was back in the clubhouse."

Pauline shrugged. "So?"

"Erick was unaccounted for at least half an hour while Ruddy was out on the golf course and then killed."

She looked into her glass. "Oh."

"The police want to question Erick."

"About Ruddy?"

"Lots of other people have alibis," I said. "Lots of other people can account for their every minute after Ruddy stormed out of here. There aren't many suspects who were missing for longer than half an hour."

"But, why would Erick want to kill Ruddy?" Pauline asked. "Erick doesn't have a motive."

Shoot. I hadn't thought this through. "Well, at this point,

A Murder at the Country Club

I think the police are looking at people who *could* have done it, who have a hole in their alibis. Everybody here told the police who they were with and when, and there's about half an hour where Erick was missing."

Pauline gulped her punch.

"I think the police might arrest him tonight," I said.

"But he didn't do it," she insisted.

"They don't know that."

Pauline glanced across the room. "I was with him during the time he was supposedly missing."

I followed her line of sight. Her husband, Tom, was leaning against the bar quite far away, talking to Maurice.

She whispered, "We sneaked upstairs to his office to be alone."

"And you were there with him the whole time?"

She nodded, tears springing to her eyes. "We've never done anything like that here at the club during an event. We always met during work hours, when no one would suspect anything. We were always careful so no one would find out."

"Sneaking out of an event together seems pretty risky," I said.

Pauline nodded. "When I came back into the clubhouse, Ruddy almost ran me over when he stomped out. I was upset, so I had a few drinks. Erick had some, too. We were reckless. We were gone for about half an hour. That's the time he was missing."

"Ann Carmo said that *you* were gone for at least forty-five minutes," I said, pushing Pauline to explain her alibi more.

"How would she know?" Pauline shot back. "She was out on the golf course the whole time. She didn't come back to the clubhouse forever, it seemed like."

I paused. "She was?"

Pauline nodded. "Ann lost her glowing golf ball on the sixteenth. You know how obsessive she is about shiny things like that. We looked for ten minutes, but she insisted that we should go on inside without her. I was horrified later that she had been out on the course in the dark with the murderer."

This wasn't making sense. "When did she shower and change clothes?"

"After she got back, I suppose. Hopefully, she wasn't out there for too long. It's scary to think that the murderer might have gotten her instead of Ruddy." She grimaced. "Especially since we left her out there alone."

"How many groups were behind you and Uncle Arnie?" I asked her.

"We were pretty much the last group in."

I sucked down a decent gulp of my drink. "I need to talk to somebody. Don't go anywhere."

Though Ann and Erick were nowhere in the bar area, I had seen Oliver Shwetz over by the bar, near Pauline's husband.

What I had to say to Oliver had nothing to do with Pauline and Erick, so I walked over. "Hey, Oliver."

A Murder at the Country Club

He turned his chubby back to me and went back to talking to his wife, who peeked around his shoulder with wide, surprised eyes.

I asked the back of Oliver's collar, "Did you see the newspaper article where Ann Carmo threw you to the wolves?"

He turned around to face me. "I beg your pardon?"

I leaned on the bar and waved to the bartender. "Maurice? Do you by any chance still have that newspaper I dropped here earlier?"

He grimaced but fished it out of the recycling bin.

I flipped the paper open to Lale's article and handed it to Oliver. "Take a gander at that last part."

Oliver Shwetz read the last few paragraphs where Ann Carmo had told Lale Kollen that she had been afraid of Oliver's terrible temper when he had been her lawyer.

I said, "She confirmed in this article that you were her lawyer, so that's now public knowledge. She made it sound like you weren't her lawyer anymore, though."

Oliver glanced at me, his dark eyes angry. "I cannot discuss matters that are under attorney-client privilege."

"So, she is or was your client. She's throwing you under the bus, Oliver. She's counting on you not to say anything. She's going to implicate you for Ruddy's murder."

"I didn't do it," Oliver said. "I've already given the police my fingerprints. They'll rule me out soon."

"But the fingerprints might not matter. Anyone's

fingerprints could have been on that knife if it was dirty, and the murderer might have worn gloves. That kind of evidence supports the theory, but it's not enough to eliminate you as a suspect."

"I cannot comment," he grated out from between clenched teeth.

I went in for a very quiet, whispered attack with my eyes wide open. "She's going to crucify you in public. You were missing during the time of the murder. You went upstairs to my office. You could have gone right down the back stairs, grabbed one of the steak knives from a bussing bin in the kitchen, and gone out to the course through that exit next to the pro shop. After that, it would have been easy for you to walk through the fifteenth hole to the parking lot. No one would have seen you if you'd gone around that way."

"I didn't do it. The police will exonerate me. I cannot discuss privileged information," Oliver snarled.

"Ruddy argued with you in public right before someone killed him. The police will have to do something, unless there's better evidence that someone else did it."

Oliver Shwetz scowled at the newspaper again.

"What did Ruddy Agani say to you when you were arguing?" I asked him.

"Privileged."

"Why was he so mad?"

"Privileged."

"You're going to go to jail for murder. You need to tell

people what happened."

His wife touched his arm and read the newspaper article, though the paper was quivering in his hand. She asked him, "Does this have something to do with the ethics committee inquiry?"

His scowl deepened. "Beth, don't say anything else."

"The ethics committee inquiry was for telling Agani something about your client during the argument." Beth Shwetz turned to me and spoke in a hurried, low voice. "I won't have my husband going to jail for something he didn't do."

"Beth, *stop*," Oliver said. "It still counts against me if you say it."

"It's still better than murder charges." She looked straight at me, resolute in what she was doing. "Ann Carmo has been Ollie's client for years. She instructed Ollie to send a threatening letter to the club when her invoices weren't paid on time. The club was three months in arrears."

"*Ann Carmo* was sending *invoices* to the club?" I whispered to Beth, thinking that yes, Ruddy had always responded badly to threatening letters from attorneys. I'd heard stories.

She said, "Ann knew that they had been approved because she was on the committee that approved them."

"Because she was approving her own invoices," I said.

Some of the names of the shell corporations came back to me.

Wilber and Friends, LLC.

Ann's husband was named Wilber Carmo.

Carmo.

Good grief, one of the shell companies had been named *Shipmo.*

Not a *car*-mo but *ship*-mo, because they had been embezzling from a *yacht* club.

It was as if Ann wanted to get caught.

It was like she was doing it for the thrill as much as the money, to laugh at the people who were blindly paying her invoices.

Like the Canterbury Golf Club.

Real, true anger lifted in my gut.

I asked Oliver, "Who else have you talked to about this?"

"I can neither confirm nor deny—"

I turned. "Beth?"

She said, "Erick Walters called two days ago, asking about the corporations. He said that the checks had been sent to Oliver's office to be passed on, so he knew Oliver had something to do with it."

Oliver looked outraged. "How did you know that?"

Beth's lips were set in a firm line. "Ollie, I keep telling you to wear your hearing aids. Then, you wouldn't have to put your cell phone on speaker so that everyone in the house can hear it."

"Beth, the police are going to want to talk to you," I told her, and at that point, I was only talking to her. "How do you know that Oliver didn't kill Ruddy that night?"

Her chin lifted. Beth had this figured out, too. "He called me from his cell phone from your office, directly after the argument and right after he texted Ann that he'd slipped and told Ruddy that he was passing the checks on to her."

Things began to slip into place in my head. "*Wait.* He *texted* Ann that night, right after the argument?"

Beth continued, "I didn't come to your glow-ball tournament because I had a summer cold. Sorry, darling. I told him to come home and talked to him every minute, from walking down the back stairs to the parking lot, to when he was driving, until he pulled into the garage. He was distraught, and I didn't want him to get in a road-rage wreck."

"I'm not sure how finely the police can track a cell phone's whereabouts, but the timestamp might be important. Where was he the night Lale Kollen was murdered?"

Beth pressed her mouth in a prim smile. "She called the house that afternoon and upset him again with all her questions. I didn't want him to stew in it, so I took him with me to bridge night. All the ladies were so happy to see a *man* at bridge night that they posted selfies with him on their social media."

"*Nice.* I need to talk to Erick," I said. "Do you know where he went?"

Beth's eyes became unfocused, and her gaze floated

somewhere above my head. "I'm not sure. You might ask Pauline Damir if she's seen him. No reason."

Wow, everyone knew about Pauline and Erick's affair but me. I was always the last to know everything.

"I'll ask her. Thanks."

Chapter 33

More people had come into the clubhouse for the Nine and Dine, and I skedaddled across the dining room again to where Pauline was talking to Trudi and Priscilla Sauveterre about the nine holes of golf they were about to play. I asked the group, "Hey, have any of you seen Erick Walters?"

Their confused looks and necks craning above the crowd told me that none of them had been keeping tabs on him.

I asked, "Do any of you happen to have his phone number? Trudi, we're on the operating budget committee with him."

Trudi tugged her phone from her immense purse—I do not know how she finds anything in that black pit of a purse of hers—and scrolled through the contacts. "I just have his email."

"Priscilla? Pauline?" I asked. "Anybody know it?"

Come to think of it, I hadn't seen either Erick or Ann for a while.

Pauline had her phone out, too, and she tapped the screen. "Oh! Look at that. I do have it. Must have been from when we were on the social committee." She held the phone to her ear and pointed at it. "It's ringing."

We waited, looking at Pauline.

Pauline bit her lower lip, looking back at all of us while she held the phone against the side of her head. "He's not answering."

"What's his number?" I said, leaning and looking at her phone. I tapped his digits into my phone and tapped it to call.

My phone rang.

And rang.

"Darny doodles, he's not—" But the ringing in my ear stopped. "Hello, Erick?"

Priscilla cocked her head to the side. "Why is it so imperative that we call him?"

Quiet voices mumbled in my phone, but no one answered my greeting.

I looked straight up at Pauline. "You're sure that's Erick's number?"

She nodded, her eyes widening.

I tapped my phone to put it on speaker mode and pressed it against my head, closing my eyes to hear better, as one does.

A woman's voice said, "I said that it's none of your business."

Erick said, in a voice far away from the phone, "Put down the knife, Ann."

I tapped the phone to mute the microphone and my voice and gasped, "We have to find Erick and Ann. She's got a knife. Where did they go?"

Right then, I did something halfway smart for once in my life: I turned on the voice memo recorder app that I had used in Lale Kollen's house and began to record what we were hearing and put the phone back on speaker.

Hey, even a retired kindergarten teacher gets it right once in a while.

We all bent our heads around my phone, cupping the phone with our hands to amplify the voices.

I just barely heard Erick say, "I haven't been in this office since the night of the glow-ball tournament."

I looked at Pauline.

Her eyes were huge, but Pauline said, "They're in Ruddy's office."

"That's odd," Trudi said. "Why would the club's treasurer not go to his own office since—"

I ran.

With my phone braced against my head, I sprinted toward the stairs. Clomping followed me, and I turned to see Trudi and Pauline hot on my heels as we ran through the dining room, dodging people. We ducked around and behind the club's glass trophy case and into the area behind it because that passage was less crowded than the main floor, where people were walking between the dining tables.

Over my phone, Erick said, "Now, Ann. We can talk about this. We can work this out."

Ann's voice said, "I need you to give me Ruddy Agani's notes right now. You don't have concrete evidence for anything. I just want those notes."

I ran faster. Pauline and Trudi kept up right behind me.

I didn't want to alert the whole club that yet another murder was about to happen, especially with the *Canterbury Tales* reporter who had identified herself as Wendy Mack standing right by the bar and watching us with widening eyes, but we ran right past Constable Sherwood Kane.

I grabbed his arm, and he stumbled but fell in with us.

"What's going on?" he asked as we reached the stairs.

"Erick Walters and Ann Carmo got upstairs somehow. She's been embezzling from the club, and now she's threatening Erick with a knife!" I said as I sprinted up the stairs. My side hurt before we got to the first landing.

"What!" Sherwood yelled as we ran. "You were supposed to stop poking your nose in where you—"

"This is not the time! Do you have your gun?"

"I don't own a gun! I'm not a cop, just an elected constable!"

I ran faster. Our footsteps thundered in the stairwell. "You should have a gun. Why wouldn't you have a gun?"

"And I certainly wouldn't concealed-carry at a country club Nine and Dine!"

A Murder at the Country Club

"Well, this is the Canterbury Golf and Murder Club, so maybe you should!"

At the top of the stairs, I grabbed the door and flung it open, and we all barreled down the hallway.

On my phone, I heard Erick ask, "Are you going to stab me like you did Ruddy and that newspaper reporter?"

Oh, all the cats and dogs in Heaven, Erick was trying to get Ann to confess while she was holding a knife on him and didn't even know whether anyone was listening or coming to save him at all. That was pretty impressive.

Ann said, "I need Ruddy's notes. No one has to get hurt. We can even work out a deal. With Ruddy writing the checks, there was too big of a risk that I would get caught. If I approve the invoices and then you write the checks, we could both make some money, and there would be even less chance of us getting caught."

I told Sherwood, "She just confessed to the embezzlement, and she didn't deny killing Lale Kollen and Ruddy Agani when he asked!"

Erick said, "Yes, we should talk about cutting me in on your plan. So, what would my percentage be? Fifty percent?"

"*Fifty!*" Ann retorted. "I've set it all up. I made it work. I'm taking all the risk. I was thinking more like five percent."

Sherwood scowled and turned on the gas, easily pulling ahead of Trudi, Pauline, and I with those stupid, long legs of his.

"Now we're just haggling," Erick said, and he chuckled.

"So why don't you put down that knife?"

We were almost to Ruddy's office.

Ann said, "Or, maybe I don't want to split the money at all. It was pretty easy to stick a knife in Ruddy and that reporter. What's one more?"

Sherwood reached Ruddy's office door and pounded beside the nameplate. "Open up!"

On my phone, Ann said, "Who's that?"

I reached him and began fumbling in my purse.

Trudi ran up beside us, but she already had her keys out and shoved one in the lock, twisting it.

Sherwood pushed the door open. "Stop! Put the knife down!"

In the middle of the room, Ann Carmo was indeed holding a long kitchen knife, her hand cocked above her head like she was about to attack.

Erick had been holding his hands up, and with all of us piling into the room, he lunged for Ann's knife.

So did Sherwood.

So did Pauline, shrieking, "You leave Erick alone!"

Trudi and I were in the back, so we watched the pile-on, horrified.

A masculine voice shouted, and then thumps and scuffling pounded the air in the room.

Sherwood slammed Ann Carmo against a wall.

Erick sat on the floor and held his bleeding arm while Pauline fussed over him. "I couldn't remember the reporter's name," he said, gasping. "I kept trying to get her to confess, but I couldn't remember the reporter's name."

"It's okay," Pauline told him. "You did great. It's okay."

Trudi and I looked at each other. She said, "Well, I guess that's it."

Wendy Mack and Priscilla Sauveterre scooted into the office last.

The newspaper reporter raised her cell phone and flashed a picture. "Anybody dead?"

"Nope," I said. "We caught the person who killed Ruddy Agani and Lale Kollen, and she was embezzling money from us and the Gnostic Yacht Club."

Wendy Mack thumbed text into her phone. "Now we've got ourselves a story."

CHAPTER 34

THE CANTERBURY POLICE station was the other half of the
Town Hall building, and everyone who had been involved in
that fiasco needed to be interviewed.

Ann Carmo was expected to be charged with the
kidnapping and assault of Erick Walters to keep her in jail
over the weekend. Charges for the two murders and
embezzlement would likely be lodged against her on
Monday morning.

There weren't too many witnesses this time, but I ended
up in Constable Kane's office instead of the police station.

I suspected that he might be looking out for me.

The Nine and Dine had been postponed until the next
week, of course. Chef Leo had stormed around the club's
kitchen like a madman when Trudi had told him, ranting
about how all the food was going to waste, until she told him
that the club would reimburse him.

Constable Kane came in and set his phone on a little

stand. He tapped the screen a couple of times. "I have to video this."

"Of course," I said.

Sherwood stated his name, and we went through the events of the evening as I recalled it. He took a few notes, but he just nodded solemnly through most of it.

When I was done recounting the tale, Sherwood leaned back in his chair, chewing the end of his pen. "So, that's how Ann knew Ruddy was out on the golf course, because Oliver texted her before he called his wife. We'll confirm that with the phone records."

"Of course."

"But I don't get how she already had a knife when she was just out there playing golf," Sherwood mused. "It looked like someone must have gone out after him. Wouldn't she have had to come back inside to get one?"

"I've been thinking about that." I picked at a hangnail on my thumb. "I think Ann is a kleptomaniac. She stole my bumblebee golf ball and the one that Trudi gave me with the little pink hearts on it. When she and I were laying out the decorations for the Nine and Dine, a bunch of silverware was missing afterward. The club's hostess even said we were going to need to order some new silverware place settings because the silverware just walked off so often. I think Ann had already stolen a steak knife just because, and that's why she had it with her."

Sherwood nodded. "That's not bad. It would explain her

house."

"Her house?"

He looked at the ceiling. "You ever see a magpie's nest? Her house wasn't like a hoarder's, where there's just stuff and stuff and piles and piles lying around. It's more like a serial killer's trophies. There were fifty spoons lying on the sideboard, lined up neatly, and a mound of golf balls in a bowl on the coffee table."

"Wow," I said.

"Yeah," he said. "We arrested her husband, Wilber, on the embezzlement charges, too. His signature was on the shell companies' incorporation forms, and he came and got her dirty golf clothes from her car trunk on the night of the glow-ball tournament, just in case the police searched the cars."

"Oh, right. Ann showered and changed clothes after the tournament. Afterward, she was wearing that long, black evening gown but no make-up. I didn't even recognize her at first without her red lipstick. She must have gotten some of Ruddy's blood on her when she stabbed him."

"Wilber has been charged as an accessory after the fact, too. He told us that he burned her clothes after he got home because 'something' had stained them."

"Oh, and that's why she didn't change into her golf shoes to go out on the course, because Wilber had already picked them up. And she got those new, bright red golf shoes after he burned her old ones. I didn't even think of all this."

"Yeah, I didn't, either. It didn't even register that night. I think that she didn't expect to change clothes. Wilber said that they'd been up to the symphony in Hartford the night before and she'd changed clothes to drive home. The murder didn't seem pre-meditated, just opportunistic."

"Right," I said. "What I want to know is—"

"I probably can't tell you."

"—why the fingerprints on the knife didn't match the fingerprints that she had on file with the police department."

"Oh," Sherwood said, "that's just a matter of record. The school district only started running those background checks ten years ago. She quit before that."

I smacked myself in the forehead. "I ruled out anyone who had worked for the school district, ever. That's why I didn't think of her. Dang it, I messed that up."

"Yeah, well," he leaned in, "I'm not official law enforcement, just an elected official, so I can say off the record that our small town could use some sprucing up in that area. There were a few things they dropped in favor of policing the tourist beaches for parking ticket income."

I laughed, but said, "Speaking of money—"

"Yeah?"

"I thought Lale Kollen killed Ruddy because she was going to inherit."

"That didn't pan out," Sherwood said.

"So who does inherit?"

"His wife, Linda, should have rights of survivorship.

However, if it turns out that she doesn't get it, his last beneficiary in case of a family tragedy is Virginia Cohen, who lives over on Pink Myrtle Street."

"She'll fill up the emergency food pantry and give it to war refugees."

"Probably," he agreed.

"But Linda should probably get it for putting up with him all these years."

"That's the truth," he said, fiddling with his pen. "Say, I'm sorry I told you to back off."

I shrugged. "It wasn't very smart of me to poke my nose into a murder investigation. Look at what happened to Lale Kollen."

He nodded. "I'm glad nothing like that happened to you."

"Thanks, Sherwood," I said.

"If we're ever around the CGC clubhouse early in the morning, maybe we could chat over coffee."

Surely, coffee wouldn't be too much to ask. "I'd like that."

CHAPTER 35

THE NEXT WEEK, the Ladies' League tee times were fully booked for our nine o'clock shotgun start.

Light clouds filled the sky, cooling the air but not threatening rain. The air looked hazy, like happiness suffused the whole club.

I strode out onto the practice putting green and grabbed the microphone from Sherlynne. All the faces looking back at me were white-streaked with sunscreen, and most of the women were wearing broad hats.

For once, they were *silent*.

Yeah, they wanted to hear what I had to say.

I cleared my throat and switched on the mic. "Good morning, ladies."

No one said a word.

"We have a shotgun start this fine morning, and we have threesomes starting at all eighteen holes. Today's game is net score and total putts, so keep track of both. Your handicaps should be noted on your scorecard. Make sure you know what hole number you're starting at. Walkers, please hang back a few minutes so that the ladies with carts can zip along the cart paths ahead of you. We've put cart people starting at the farthest holes."

Still, no one spoke.

No one moved, either.

The people who were walking shifted their weight and watched me.

The riders stared from inside their little carts.

"All right," I said. "Go ahead. Who wants to ask?"

Nell Rinaldi's hand shot up. "Are the police sure Ann Carmo did it?"

"She won't talk to the police, and she is trying to find a new lawyer, too. It seems that her old one won't take her calls. However, the police have her confession recorded from my cell phone. Constable Sherwood said that her fingerprints match the unidentified ones on both knives. I think that's about as good as anyone could ask for."

Voices rumbled from the crowd.

"Anybody else?" I asked.

A woman in the back, Sun-Ling, asked, "So, it's safe now?"

"Perfectly safe," I reassured her and the half of the league who were probably wondering the same thing. "It looks like Ann was responsible for both murders and the embezzlement. She's awaiting an arraignment. Constable

Kane says that it doesn't look like she'll be allowed bail."

The league sighed with relief.

"Okay?" I asked. "Can we get back to business? Have a good round, ladies. Good luck."

The golf carts chugged down the cart path toward the far holes, and I gave Sherlynne back the microphone before I walked over to where Trudi and Moonie were waiting. "We're starting at the third hole."

Trudi grinned at me and shoved her enormous, four-wheeled pushcart to get it moving. Her clubs might be cut down for her size, but she had every golf toy ever made in her bag and cart, and I suspected a few other things, too. "It's a good day. I get my monthly BLT today, too."

"Are you staying for lunch, Moonie?" I asked.

"Yes," she said, her voice resolute. "I am staying for lunch, and I will eat a sandwich."

I smiled at Moonie, who had many struggles but seemed to be doing well that day.

We were all doing well that day, as the women of Ladies' League trotted out to their assigned holes for a lovely, cheery, non-murdery day of golf.

Beatrice Yates might have solved this murder,
but everything goes to heck
at the Canterbury Golf Club's annual Halloween
party,
The Devil's Ball.

CPSIA information can be obtained
at www.ICGtesting.com
Printed in the USA
LVHW032344220320
650870LV00006B/1715

9 781692 070809